BURNER

FROM THE ADVENTURES OF H.B. FIST

R. Scott Bolton

Copyright 2018 by R. Scott Bolton
ISBN: 978-0-9997962-0-7
A Rough Edge Studios Production
www.roughedgestudios.com

This book is dedicated to my favorite author, the late Robert B. Parker. Each time I read a Parker novel, I can't wait to sit down and write. His novels delight and inspire me. If you haven't read any of his novels and you're thinking about purchasing this one, put this one down and buy his instead. You'll thank me later. (Please don't forget to buy this one next time).

This book is also dedicated to my wife Shelley, who puts up with more than you can imagine but love is a two-way street, ain't it, baby?

And, as always, thanks to my continuing and ever growing panel of proof readers and advice gurus. The opinions of the following people helped guide and form this book before it got into your hands so, as always, they share the credit and the blame equally. Thanks, Team Fist: Shelley Bolton, Doug Bolton, John DeRuvo, James DeRuvo, Jeff Rogers, Steve Snider and my late friend Keith Guyotte, whose goofy smile I will miss.

Other books by R. Scott Bolton

From the Adventures of H. B. Fist
KILLED BY DEATH
OVERNIGHT SENSATION

CHAPTER ONE

The world around me was *alive*.

I was cradled in the emerald womb of a teeming jungle. Tentacles of rope-like vines, packed so densely they blocked out most of the sunlight, reached down from the tops of towering, moss-covered trees. A thick carpet of tangled vegetation, spongy grass and dead leaves hugged the landscape as far as the eye could see – which wasn't very far at all thanks to the tightly bunched greenery and subsequent lack of daylight.

The trills and cries of countless animal inhabitants filled the air. Lions. Tigers. Bears. Oh, my. All of them were hunting for something to eat in order to survive. Some hunted for plants, some for insects, some for other animals.

Some were probably hunting for me.

I took a deep breath, inhaling the musky scent of moist soil and rotting leaves mixed with the cool freshness of clean, untainted air. The elephantine trunks of the giant trees that towered above me slammed down into the Earth as if God himself had planted them there – not by dropping tiny seeds into a welcoming earth but rather by spiking them into the ground like mammoth spears.

I had no idea where I was, but I could tell that I was hours, if not days, from any form of civilization.

BURNER

The sounds of the jungle gently rocked me with their purity and I relaxed and basked in the glory of nature. I didn't know where I was and I had no memory of how I got there, yet still I felt peaceful and calm. Perhaps it was the tranquilizing effect of simply existing amidst God's most natural creations or perhaps I was so burned-out by "modern" society that this complete absence of civilization was like a soma. It didn't matter what the reason. I took another breath of the intoxicating sweet outdoors air and felt my lungs drink up its life-giving effervescence.

Somewhere in the distance, a flock of birds beat their wings in unison and suddenly bolted into the sky from the tree they'd been sleeping in. I strained to see them but could not; the trees and brush were too closely packed to grant me any sight of the skyline. I wondered if something had spooked them or if they had just decided as a community that it was time to move on.

Something cracked like a broken bone and the booming *kee-rack!* echoed throughout the forest like a cannon shot. More birds broke for cover and fled into the sky. This time I saw them as they passed directly over me, blocking what little sky peeked through the interwoven treetops with the furious fluttering of their feathered wings.

There was no longer any question as to the reasoning behind their retreat. Something had disturbed them. I just didn't know what it was. A little ooze of cold fear dripped into the pit of my stomach. Should I be spooked as well?

Or was I safe here, in the very heart of Mother Nature.

There was another crack, not quite as loud as the first, and for the first time I became aware that something was coming toward me. Something huge. I could hear small brush being slapped aside and the tiny snaps of branches breaking. Underneath those sounds of destruction, I could hear a heavy, rasping breath being drawn in and exhaled.

I didn't stand, but I craned my neck and straightened my back to try and peer into the dense forest. Still, I could see nothing.

But I could hear *it* coming.

I could hear its steps, slow and *very* heavy, as more brush was crushed and more branches broken beneath what must be mighty feet.

A cluster of trees directly before me began to shake nervously. They shook slowly at first, hardly moving at all, and then they begin to shiver like a child in the cold. A moment later, then began to vibrate wildly, their leaves and branches whipping against one another, until the thrashing became so violent that they couldn't possibly stay rooted any longer.

Then, with an explosive crash, the trees were suddenly flattened. I watched as they were driven to the ground and pinned there as something huge and heavy stood on their fallen trunks.

And I saw what it was that had scared the birds.

It looked like a dinosaur of some kind, yet unlike any dinosaur I had ever seen. Its skin was a scaly blue-ish hide

3

that rolled with scars, boils and dark blotches. Beneath that skin rippled layers of knotted muscle, trembling with barely restrained power. It stood on two legs and dragged behind it a powerful prehensile tail that was nearly as long as its body. It had the arms and shoulders of a man, a broad chest and bulging biceps. Its neck triangled up to its head which was also like a man's ... and yet not. Needle-like teeth filled its glistening maw like tightly packed fence posts. Its black tongue licked out and swept around its rough, cracked lips. Its eyes were like two scarabs set into the stone wall of its square-jawed head. Tiny pupils, blacker on black, scanned the area before them.

And its sharp-taloned claws were dripping with thick, crimson blood.

Something else's blood.

The thing muscled through the trees and straightened to its full height. It arched its back and sniffed for prey.

That trickle of fear in my belly became a rushing stream. I watched the horrible beast, not knowing whether to run, to remain still where I was or to cry out for help. It seemed the only thing I could do was wait.

The pin-pricks that were the thing's pupils suddenly snapped forward and its scaled nostrils flared wide. A swaying stalactite of saliva oozed out of its mouth and bungeed slowly to the leaf-carpeted ground.

And then the monster looked directly at me.

A chill of cold fear knifed through me. The beast had found me and I knew that it would come for me. But still I sat and watched. Still I sat and felt my fear grow deeper and colder.

The beast took a step forward. Then another. Creeping closer. The ground shook with its every step. As it neared, I could see other details: Spatters of blood on its lips, pieces of torn flesh hanging from between its needle teeth. Again, its nostrils twitched anxiously.

Closer it came. I could smell it now - the odor of old garbage and animal carcasses. I could see caked soil firmly encrusted between its scales and I knew how much pain that must have caused. Terrible pain. Maddening pain.

And I could see the insane hunger in its eyes.

The beast took two more steps and then it was on me. It opened its enormous maw and I found myself staring up into a gullet that seemed infinite. I could smell the meaty stench of death on its hot breath.

And then someone politely tapped my shoulder.

"Mr. Fist?" a voice whispered. "Mr. Fist, excuse me, sir..."

I jerked my head away from the needle-mouthed monster and it vanished instantly. The world around it vanished, too.

In its place, a large circular room appeared. Two hundred other people sat in padded chairs there, staring up in horror at the invisible image that was being projected directly into their mind's eye.

All except me. I was staring at a pimply-faced usher in a polyester tuxedo who looked down at me nervously. The flashlight in his hands ended in a red cone that made it look like a laserblade.

"I'm sorry to interrupt your MindFlick, Mr. Fist," the usher said. "But there's a call for you. They said it was urgent."

I glanced from the usher to Candy, my wife, sitting beside me. She stared into the air above her head, wide-eyed and completely engrossed. I wondered what she was seeing. Since my MindFlick had been suddenly interrupted, I could only guess.

"Damn well better be urgent," I grumbled, standing. "It was just getting good."

"The manager said he'd refund your money, sir," the usher said quickly. "I'm very sorry to interrupt you."

I followed him up the aisle toward a door tagged with a big glowing EXIT sign. "Don't worry about it," I told him. "Now where's this call?"

CHAPTER TWO

As I followed the nervous teenaged usher to the theater's companel, I wondered who would be calling me. Obviously, as the usher had said, it had to be urgent. First, nobody would be willing to risk my wrath by interrupting a MindFlick that I had paid good money for with some minor emergency. Second, the manager of the MindFlick theater would have had to be convinced that the call was important enough to interrupt a MindFlick in progress. That just wasn't done.

Except, of course, when it really *was* urgent.

So what the hell was going on?

The usher led me to a door marked "Manager" and knocked lightly. "Come in," someone said from inside, and the usher pushed the door open and extended his arm, inviting me in.

A man sat behind the faded yellow metal desk there, sweating profusely. The chair he sat in was threadbare; the desk itself covered with manila folders and blue-lined yellow writing pads. His black polyester tuxedo was stretched tautly around his rotund torso like a balloon skin. The chipped and faded nametag on his chest was barely legible: "Stanley Eisen, Manager."

Mr. Eisen struggled off his chair and wobbled toward me. "Mr. Fist, I'm sorry to bother you, sir, but you have an urgent call." He pointed at an antique companel on the desk and I squeezed past him and grabbed up the receiver.

"Fist."

"Thank God, H.B." I recognized the voice immediately and a wave of foreboding flooded over me. If Boris Cushing was calling me out of a MindFlick, something serious was indeed afoot.

"Can you go FV?" Boris asked. His voice seemed different; thicker than usual. Strained. My anxiety level crept up another notch.

I looked down at the old companel and tried to locate the Full Video switch. The buttons were broken and brown with age and where painted labels might have once been were now only blurry smears. I motioned to the manager who hurried over.

"FV?"

"Right here, sir."

He pushed a jagged half-button that had apparently broken several years ago. The oily grime of a thousand different fingers clung to the broken plastic like gum chewed too long and left under a fast food restaurant table. There was a sickly rattling noise and, finally, the wall before me flickered and the image of Boris Cushing appeared there.

It was all I could do not to gasp out loud.

Boris and I had been friends for many years. He was the man who signed my paychecks. I'd known him since he'd first approached me about mercenary work during the last years of the Zombie Slave Wars. Boris was huge, topping the scales at over 1100 pounds. A complicated series of custom scaffolds and pulleys kept him upright and allowed him limited movement. Yet, despite all that extra weight and added machinery, Boris had always looked healthy. Robust. Hearty.

Today he looked like shit.

His hair was tousled as though he used an eggbeater this morning instead of a brush. His clothes were rumpled and appeared to have been slept in. Even his weight-assisting machinery looked out of sync and cock-eyed as though he had forced it into place too quickly. And his face was a pasty shade of off-white that I had never seen before. He looked like a man who had just seen a ghost.

His own ghost.

"Boris, what the hell …?"

Boris took a deep breath that caught in his throat on chunks of emotion. Even though the cheap companel image wasn't the best quality, I swore I could almost see tears in his eyes.

Tears!

"They blew it up, H.B.," he finally managed, his voice hitching like a fifteen year old's. "The bastards blew it up."

"Blew what up?"

"The Memorial," Boris croaked, his voice breaking again. "They blew up the ZSW Memorial. It's gone. At least three thousand people are dead."

His words hit me like a sledgehammer, slamming into my chest, the impact wobbling my legs beneath me. I reached back, my fingers scrabbling for any purchase. When they found something, I pulled the ratty chair beneath me and fell back into it, my heart suddenly pounding. My whole body felt as though someone had flipped the "off" switch and I was going numb, from the tips of my toes to the top of my head. I felt like an inflatable doll whose air had just been let out in one violent blast.

"I just got a call from Washington," Boris continued. "The attack happened just minutes ago. They think maybe it was an Inferno bomb. Took the whole thing out in a second."

"Inferno bombs are blocked by the Earthshield," I said numbly.

"That's just a preliminary report."

Suddenly, my head fell into my hands. The loss I felt was like an icy cinderblock in my chest. The ZSW Memorial destroyed? Why? And by whom? What sick bastard would destroy the most precious gathering place of the families of those who had given the ultimate sacrifice? What insane son of a bitch would wipe out a testament to the triumph of good over evil?

And who the fuck would take the lives of three thousand innocent people?

I forced myself to look up at the image of Boris while another emotion began to creep maliciously into my body. Grief and horror were forced out of the way as something stronger and more dangerous swelled throughout me.

"Who did this?" My voice was asphalt and gravel and it barely slithered out from between my tightly clenched teeth.

"We don't know," Boris said. "No one's claimed responsibility yet."

"They will. Nobody's going to pull off an atrocity like this and not crow about it." I took another deep breath, hoping it would stabilize my furious state of mind. It didn't. It didn't even come close.

"I want in on this, Boris," I growled. "I want in at the top. I want to know everything as it happens."

"The President's already asked for you." Boris took a deep breath, as though trying to cleanse the horror from his mind. I could tell from the way his body shuddered that it wasn't working. He choked, a split second away from a sob. "I want you to find these bastards and flapjack them for all eternity," he said slowly. "I want them gone forever."

An awful sneer formed across my face and I felt every muscle in my body tighten angrily. The shock and horror hadn't passed – it would take months or maybe even years for that – but they had moved to the back of the bus to allow Big Daddy to step forward. White rage surged through me like a wildfire in my blood.

"Flapjacking's too good for these bastards," I said. "I'm on my way."

And snapped off the connection.

CHAPTER THREE

The way I see it, it must have happened something like this:

Corrin Nethers was only four years old when her father was sent off to fight in the Zombie Slave War. Although she loved her daddy dearly, Corrin wasn't afraid or even very sad when Kevin Nethers shipped out. Kevin had promised her that he would see her soon. And Corrin knew that daddy always told the truth.

Even though Maryanne, Corrin's mother, was trying bravely not to cry when her husband made that promise to their daughter, Corrin knew that she'd see her daddy as soon as he finished fighting the bad guys.

It was only four months later that the man with the beige uniform and dark sunglasses showed up at the Nethers' doorstep. Corrin had answered the door and smiled up at the stoic gentleman with the smooth skin and sharply angled jaw. Corrin had been dazzled by the shiny gold medals that clung to the man's chest in clusters.

"Hello, honey," the man had said in a voice as smooth as his skin. "Is your mommy home?"

"Yes," Corrin replied, standing still, staring at the man's crisply pressed pants and eyeing his chest full of glittering metal.

"Can you get her for me, honey? It's kind of important."

"Yep." Corrin had skipped away, leaving the front door open, and ran to find her mother. Maryanne was in the kitchen, making a peanut butter sandwich for her daughter.

"There's a man here to see you, mommy," Corrin said.

"A man ...?" Maryanne began. And then her voice closed up and, years later, Corrin would understand that it was then that her mother knew. Maryanne dropped the knife onto the table, pressed the sandwich into Corrin's hand, and walked quickly to the front door. She didn't run, Corrin remembered, but she walked rapidly toward the door as if hoping to see a Bible salesman there instead of a man in a military uniform.

But it *was* a man in a military uniform. And he didn't smile when Maryanne approached the door.

"Yes?" Maryanne whispered.

"Mrs. Kevin Nethers?" the man asked kindly.

"Yes."

"I'm Sergeant William Spano from the Global Alliance Military Forces," he said softly. "I'm afraid I have some bad news."

Sitting at the table eating her sandwich, four-year-old Corrin Nethers stopped chewing when she heard her mommy sob out loud from the front room. She put down her sandwich and crept to the kitchen door, where she cautiously peered at the man and her mom.

Corrin's mommy was on her knees, her head in her hands, her body wracked with sobs. Corrin could see that her mother's apron was already wet with spilled tears. The

13

man with the crisp uniform and dark sunglasses was bending over her, his hand on her shoulder, offering a handkerchief and his best sympathetic support.

Later that night, as Maryanne tucked Corrin into bed, she told her four-year-old daughter that Daddy had been unable to keep his promise. She cried softly as she told Corrin that she would never see her Daddy again.

Five years later, with the war won and a new age dawning for the re-organized Galactic Alliance, Corrin Nethers and her mother stood near a wall of the ZSW Memorial in Washington, DC and read their father/husband's name etched in the stone there. There were nearly a million of these names but it had taken them only a few minutes to find "Kevin Nethers." The Memorial's extensive database and navigation system made it quick and easy.

Corrin, now nine years old, was finally able to understand why her father had been unable to keep his promise. He had put his life on the line to keep the world safe for Corrin, her mother, their neighbors and, in fact, everyone on the planet. Everyone in the universe. And he had given everything he had to give in the battle of good versus evil. The war had eventually been won and today the galaxy was a better place. Corrin understood now that her father was at least a little part of that improvement and, although she would have given anything to have her father back, she understood that his life was not taken in vain.

Corrin watched as Maryanne reached up and ran her

fingers across her husband's name. Corrin followed suit, touching the edges of the etched letters with her fingertips. She marveled at how they felt; rough and yet smooth at the same time. Finally, looking at her mother for approval and for strength, Corrin slid the tips of her first three fingers toward the center of her father's etched name. Maryanne placed her fingers on those of her daughter and pressed gently.

Their eyes closed involuntarily. The world seemed to fade around them as their fingertips began to buzz with a slight electrical charge.

Then, the voice was in their heads. A voice Corrin remembered from five years before.

The voice of her father.

"Hey, guys. It's me, dad. If you get this message, I guess that means I didn't make it. I'm sorry I couldn't keep my promise, Cory."

A tear slipped out of Corrin's closed eye and fell to the concrete sidewalk beneath her. Its dark stain remained for a moment, and then slowly faded away.

Tears were streaming down Maryanne's face, too, but Corrin didn't see them. Around them, thousands of others stood with their hands pressed against names on the wall, the final words and thoughts of their valiant loved ones playing through their mind's eye.

Inside Corrin's head, her father's voice seemed to bloom. The next thing she knew, although her eyes were still closed, she could see her father's face vividly. Exactly

15

as it had looked five years ago.

"This is kinda weird, talking as though I'm already de...,
um, gone," the image of Kevin Nethers continued. "But,
according to Sarge, that's why we're recording these. So, I
guess I'll just keep talking. Maryanne, I miss you already.
With any luck, I'll be back in a month or two and you'll
never see this. Whatever happens, remember that I'll
always love you and that you're always on my mind. Cory, I
love you, too. More than anything. More than the whole
wide world. Right now I've got some work to do. No
matter what happens, honey, remember this: Daddy loves
you."

The image of Kevin Nethers looked over its virtual
shoulder and nodded.

"I guess I gotta go now. I love you both and I'll see you
soon." He gave a sardonic little laugh. "Of course, if you're
looking at this, I guess I won't. Bye!"

The image faded and then vanished and Corrin's
fingers jerked away from the wall as though she'd been
shocked. She looked up at her mother, whose cheeks were
wet with tears, and they fell into each other's arms, their
embrace strengthening them both.

Around them, the soft, quiet sobs of thousands gently
filled the air.

Corrin took a deep breath and pushed gently away
from her mother. She surveyed the people around her,
feeling their pain as they remembered loved ones and
listened to voices of those long dead. She thought about

how important this memorial was. Not only as a tribute to those who died but as a reminder of the pain that war caused. She saw mothers and fathers and wives and husbands, all of whom shared a common wound and who, with this wall and the camaraderie it brought, had found strength and support in others. They were all part of the same family here.

A tiny flicker of yellow light caught Corrin's eyes, surprising her. She looked in the direction it came from and was disappointed when it faded before she could locate its source.

Down the way, a man stood, his fingers pressed tightly against several different names. For some reason - and it wasn't just the man's perfectly combed, bright orange hair – Corrin thought it looked odd. There were plenty of people pushing their fingers against the wall, listening to the voices of long dead loved ones. Some were even taking rubbings from the etched names, rubbings that they would take home and keep in memorial scrapbooks. But this man was just leaning against the wall, touching not just one name but a group of them, his fingers working against the stone like a baker kneading bread.

Maybe he doesn't know how to use the names, Corrin thought. Poor guy. She squeezed her mother's hand and stepped away, moving toward the orange-haired man. They were all friends here. They were Family. She would show him how to do it correctly.

But as she got closer, Corrin noticed that the man

17

wasn't just pushing against the wall with his fingers. He was actually pushing some sort of rubbery substance, like gum, into the names thereon. The substance filled the names and oozed out of them, like some sort of putty.

As Corrin stepped beside the man, she saw him pull a small, disc-shaped device from under his coat. He pressed it against the wall and held it there until it stuck firm. Then, he quickly looked up and down the hallway ...

... and locked eyes with Corrin.

"Excuse me," Corrin asked with sweet, nine-year-old innocence. "Did you need some help working the memories?"

The man's eyes widened in surprise and then he smiled. "No, hon, I'm fine." He reached into his pocket and withdrew a tiny rectangular device. "Thanks, though." He fingered the device and the yellow light twinkled again. When it faded, the man was gone.

Corrin blinked, stunned. Where had the man gone? She glanced around quickly but he was nowhere to be seen.

She turned back to the wall and stared at the names the man had been touching. She found the tiny disc the man had stuck to the wall and reached up to touch it.

As her finger neared it, the device gave a menacing little chirp.

Corrin's world flared white hot and came to a quick and decisive end.

In the space of a nano-second, the ZSW Memorial and more than three thousand visitors vanished in a blast of unimaginable heat and radioactive fire.

That quickly, the last thoughts of too damn many dead soldiers, and the lives of their surviving family members, were cruelly and instantly extinguished.

CHAPTER FOUR

It took all of my patience, not that I had a whole hell of that left, to bring the Charger to a halt and identify myself at the entrance of Camp Deckard in Washington, DC. I knew it was an essential procedure for a Multi-Military base, especially after a terrorist attack, but that cold, fiery fury was burning in my blood and I was eager to take action right now. Every minute that passed without getting started was like a needle in my eye.

Thankfully, the I.D. process didn't take too long. The guards were expecting me, gave me and the Charger a swift but thorough inspection, apologized briefly for the delay and waved me through.

I don't even remember parking the car. The next thing I knew, I had smashed open the front door of the Command Center, walked past a half dozen gawking cadets and secretaries, and barreled my way to the twin doors that led down into the War Room.

Of course, they stopped me there as well, checked my I.D. again, and x-rayed me for any illegal weapons. I offered them the flapjacker, but they gave it the usual respected berth, knowing that I would only be assigned the weapon if I were trustworthy and that its DNA encoding would render it useless to me if I wasn't its rightful owner.

I was so tense that my stomach didn't even develop the

usual sinking feeling that happens when I make the drop from ground level to 70 floors deep into the Earth. The numbers flashed by on the wall before me as the elevator dropped deeper and deeper toward the War Room.

The moment the elevator stopped, I forced my way between the sliding doors and strode directly into two heavily armed marines. They blocked my way politely yet effectively and, again, I flashed my I.D. and was inspected - both physically and with security electronics. I watched them as they ran the instruments carefully over me and I wondered, if I were one of the bad guys, could I take these two out and continue onward? I decided I probably could, if they were alone. However, I also knew that the sniper hidden in the vaulted ceiling above had me in his crosshairs and would blow my head clean off before I landed a second blow.

"You're clear, Mr. Fist," said one of the guards, deactivating his handheld security device. "Please go on in, sir."

I mumbled my thanks and pressed forward. A pair of twin doors ended a long hallway in front of me and I strode on, my feet pumping rapidly, heels clacking off the highly polished granite floor. I came to the double doors and stiff-armed them open.

The first thing I saw was Boris, sitting at one end of a long table, a sheath of papers and diagrams spread out before him. He looked a little better than he had earlier this morning, but the intense stress was obviously still affecting him. The scaffolding that he needed to stand and ambulate had been removed and put to one side. He wasn't going anywhere. He was in for the long haul.

The second thing I saw were the others, about forty of them, split evenly on opposite sides of the table, who stared up at me with looks that expressed either shock, surprise or relieved welcome.

I gave them the best smile I could muster under the circumstances, and nodded a universal greeting.

Boris gave a deep sigh of relief. "This, ladies and gentlemen ..." he told the congregation surrounding him, "... is Alliance Mercenary Horatio Bartholomew Fist."

I nodded again and took a moment to inventory those around me. The President was there, looking anxious and outraged all at once. I had always thought of him as somewhat of a buffoon, but he seemed different today. The horrendous attack had removed any traces of the fun-loving idiot the media loved to laugh at. In its place was a stern, get-to-business attitude that proved it wasn't just a pretty face that got you elected these days.

Well, most of the time at least.

The leaders of the various military branches and defense organizations were there, too, each looking just as grim and determined as the President. I recognized representatives from a few major countries and a few minor ones as well. Some of the department heads I'd met when going to Washington functions with my wife Candy were there. And I saw my old friend Sonny Beach, the Global Alliance Sheriff. He offered me a somber smile and

22

I gave him a brief wink back.

"What'd I miss?" I asked. I didn't take time for pleasantries. I wanted information and I wanted it now. Otherwise, there was the risk that these ninnies would play political pocket pool all day and the bastards who destroyed the ZSW would mince merrily away from the crime scene, free as the proverbial lark.

Boris caught my impatience and flipped back to the first few pages in his folder. "We don't have much at the mo…" he began.

"Excuse me, Mr. Cushing," someone interrupted in a cultivated, baritone voice. I turned my head to face a big-shouldered and well-dressed man sitting beside the President. A folded piece of cardboard in front of him read "Colin Hancock" and, beneath that, "Presidential Advisor." Hancock glanced my way and continued. "Mr. Fist can be briefed later. Let's not lose momentum by starting over again for someone who arrived late."

A scowl etched itself across my face as Hancock and I locked eyes and I thought back to the day that Candy had first introduced me to him. I remembered my first impression of him and it hadn't changed. He was a pompous, arrogant prick.

"Mr. Hancock," Boris said diplomatically, "Mr. Fist is going to be our man in the field here. I don't think we're 'wasting time' by briefing him now."

"I didn't ask you what you thought, Boris," Hancock said levelly, his eyes never leaving me. "I said move on."

Boris froze, embarrassed and undecided. So I took the lead. "Sorry I'm late, folks," I said, maintaining eye contact with Hancock. "But I was in California fifteen minutes ago. Please, Boris, continue from where you left off. Despite Mr. Hancock's lack of faith, I'm sure I'll be able to catch up before this meeting is adjourned."

I gave Hancock a pleasant fuck you smile and his look of haughty confidence told me he would let me get away with it. This time. He slowly looked down and made a quick note on the yellow pad there on the desk before him. Probably something nasty about me. "Fist eats boogers." Or worse.

An intern brought me a cup of coffee and led me to a chair. I quietly asked her for a Coca-Cola instead. I sat behind a small cardboard tent that had "H.B. Fist, M.O.A." printed across it in tight, black block letters.

Boris waited patiently until I sat down and then went back to his notes, flipping to the point they'd been at when I arrived. "As I started to say, we don't have much at the moment. We know that the ZSW Memorial was destroyed today at 9:51 AM by what appears at first look to be Inferno bomb technology. We don't have an exact casualty count yet, but we're estimating fatalities in the thousands, maybe as many as four thousand."

A low, angry whistle escaped from between my teeth.

"No group or individual has claimed responsibility yet but, as you said on the phone when we spoke earlier, Mr. Fist ..." Boris paused briefly and gave Hancock a quick glance to let him know that I'd been involved from the beginning. "...they will. Nobody takes this kind of action unless they want the Alliance to sit up and notice."

"How sure are we that it's an Inferno bomb?" I asked.

"General Dalton?" Boris turned to a squat, sparkplug of a man in a beige military uniform. A rainbow of ribbons lazed over the man's shoulders.

"We're about 90% certain at the moment," said Dalton. I knew Dalton from my days in the ZSW. He was the Commanding Officer of the G.A. Army and a damn fine solider. He'd aged a bit since I last saw him, of course, but he still looked healthy, hearty and ready to kick ass. His crisply pressed uniform was flawless. "Judging from aerial photographs of the blast circumference, the pattern is similar to the unique pattern of Inferno technology."

"How long before you're certain?"

"As soon as we can get over the site, we can take radiation readings and match those patterns from the air. That will either confirm or deny our suspicions. But that could be days ... maybe even weeks."

"Inferno technology isn't easy to come by," I reminded everyone.

"What, exactly, is Inferno technology?" asked a woman I didn't recognize. I read her nameplate but didn't recognize the name: Janet Sutton. I did recognize her title, however: Director, Department of Agricultural Defense.

I nodded at General Dalton and he waved me to go on. "Inferno technology is a very dangerous type of weapon in that bombs can be made that are very tiny but incredibly destructive. Basically, they burn briefly at a temperature very near that of the core of the sun," I said. "Because they're so easy to conceal and because they're so hugely destructive, they've been banned by every civilized government and military in the known galaxy. Five years ago, the EarthShields were programmed to recognize and block the bomb's active ingredient - gunspore."

"So, if it's an Inferno bomb, why didn't the 'Shields detect the gunspore?" Sutton asked.

"That's a valid question and one we'll have to answer quickly in order to prevent further attacks," I told her.

"Just a minute," Hancock interrupted, "I don't see where all this talk about Inferno bombs and gunspore is getting us."

"Gunspore is a rare and extremely unique mineral, that is also very, very expensive," I told him. "Your average terrorist couldn't afford it."

"And what does that prove?" Hancock said irritably.

"What it proves, Mr. Hancock, is that – once we know for certain it's an Inferno bomb – we can probably trace it back to its origin."

Hancock seemed momentarily flustered. He hadn't thought of that.

The President rubbed his cheek with a pencil eraser. "So if we can confirm this was an Inferno bomb," he said, "we can trace it back to whoever did this?"

"With any luck," I said.

"It's a great starting point," General Dalton added. "It won't take long to inventory every known gunspore stockpile in the Alliance. A few days at most."

"I'd suggest you put someone on that right now, Mr. President," I agreed. "We can't afford to wait even until this meeting is over."

The President nodded and turned to an aide sitting behind him. He dictated a few quiet orders and the intern took a few quick notes and raced out of the war room.

"General Dalton," I said. "Off the top of your head, can you give us a list of any countries, planets or extremist groups who might have the finances to acquire Inferno technology or gunspore?"

"There are only a handful," Dalton told us. "The Temtamoree could have, at one point, but they're pretty much out of business today. Their funding is so sub-par they can't afford a sandwich, much less gunspore. The Walshock government might have the means but, according to our latest intel, their terrorist days are behind them. We hit them so hard last time they tried something that the civilians there staged a revolution."

He took a sip of coffee and then settled back again. "There are others who'd like to, of course, but I can't think of anybody who has the funding or the ability to destroy the ZSW."

"What about Zombie Slave Traders?" Hancock said suddenly, hungrily turning his hawkish eyes back to me. "They'd have a score to settle, and they'd have the money."

"No, they wouldn't," I said evenly. "As you know ..." I glanced at Hancock. "... Well, as *most* of you know, I'm somewhat of an expert on Zombie Slave Traders. First, there isn't enough business in the slavery industry these days to drum up much funding. The G.A. has made the consequences of that source of income far too painful. Second, with the head of that particular snake firmly locked up in flapjack stasis, there's no organization." I shook my head confidently. "This isn't the work of Zombie Slave Traders."

"Any others?" the President asked.

"I'm still stunned that anyone would *dare* such an attack," I replied. "They know the sort of response the Galactic Alliance has dished out in the past. Any organization, government or individual that harbored terrorists has been smudged out."

"Maybe that's the problem," said a representative from Brazil. "Maybe we should have tried negotiating with them instead of just destroying them."

I shrugged. "Hard to negotiate with someone if you don't know who they are," I said. "And not everyone wants to negotiate. There are those who won't be satisfied until their religion is the only religion allowed in the galaxy. There are those who want the Galactic Alliance dismantled and the corporate dictatorships put back into power. There are those who think that everyone who doesn't think exactly like they do should be wiped off the face of the earth. How do you negotiate with that?"

"You don't," Hancock said.

And, for the first time, I agreed with him.

The President spoke up again. "The Galactic Alliance has a long-standing and unbreakable policy that we do not negotiate with terrorists. The only time terrorism works is when you bow to their demands."

"Looking for a political reason behind this may be barking up the wrong tree," I said. "It would take a real wacko to do a job like this. Someone who didn't care if they got caught or someone who is so cocky they think they won't get caught. For all we know, it was one guy. And he may have gone up with the Memorial."

It was quiet for a moment as everyone considered that grim possibility. "What's the next step, then?" Boris finally asked.

"Step up the intel and see what we uncover," I said. "We've got to know what type of explosive was used, how the hell it got through our security systems and who had the money, manpower, and the skills necessary to pull it off. The answers are out there, we've just got to find them."

"I want no stone unturned," said the President. He stood and addressed those at the table. "Spare no resource, ladies and gentlemen. I don't care what it takes, I want the people responsible for this atrocity brought to justice. And I want it done soon." He gently thumped his fist on the table. "You know what to do. Now, let's get moving."

As the others gathered their paperwork, I moved toward the President, who was now quietly conferring with

Hancock.

"Excuse me, sir," I said.

"Yes, Mr. Fist? What can I do for you?"

"I'd like to tour the blast site."

"So would I, Mr. Fist, but you heard General Dalton. It may be weeks before we can get close enough to garner any useable information."

"Actually," I said, "I've been thinking about that. And I think we can do it today.

CHAPTER FIVE

I've seen a lot of bad shit in my lifetime. Far too much of it. I've seen cities torn apart by war, I've seen worlds wrecked by natural disasters. I've seen ten thousand dead men, their only crime the desire to protect their homeland, stacked to the sky in a great, meaty pyramid.

But nothing I'd ever seen prepared me for the dreadful nothingness that was formerly the Zombie Slave War Memorial.

We hovered over what was basically just an angry black crater. The President and General Dalton were with me, as was Hancock. We were joined by three heavily armed secret service agents whose hidden weapons alone probably weighed more than the JL-7 Pod Runner we were traveling in. Boris, too big to fit inside, was on the companel screen.

The Pod Runner was my idea. It was designed to burrow through suns in order to research their suscepti-bility to nova and their potential as an energy source. I figured if the JL-7 could stand up to a sun, it could withstand the aftereffects of any bomb, including an Inferno bomb, if that was what we were dealing with here. A quick discussion with some of the Alliance's top engineers confirmed my theory.

A uniformed pilot stood at the controls, guiding us carefully over the horror below and keeping a sharp eye on the Runner's shield data and power supplies.

BURNER

Below us, streams of snaking smoke curled toward the sky. There was little debris. What was once a monument to bravery and a testament of peace was now nothing more than an ugly hole; a wound in the soul of the Earth.

A wound that hurt like hell.

The hollowness in my chest and belly prevented me from speaking. Staring down at the devastation, where once had stood three thousand proud but heartbroken mourners and selfless volunteers, I felt as though someone had replaced my heart with an ice cube and the chilled blood was coursing through my every vein and artery.

"How big is the crater?" I asked dully, noting that, from our vantage point, it looked as though it stretched all the way to the horizon.

"Three square miles," answered the pilot. "And the heatwave killed people as far as six miles away."

"What about the radioactivity?"

"Should be under control soon," the pilot replied. He bent low and peered up at the sky. A moment later, he pointed. "There. See 'em?"

I followed his finger and saw a dozen or so silvery spots dancing in the gloomy grey sky. "Absorption drones?"

"That's right," the pilot told me. "They're sucking up every last radioactive morsel. If you went outside now, you'd be dead in three seconds. In a week or so, when the drones are done, this place will be clean enough to farm on again. Then, we'll dump the drones into the sun."

"Fallout?"

"We're inoculating everyone within a hundred miles of this place," said the President. His voice was soft with exhaustion and rough with overuse. It had been a tough day but I was pleased with the way he was holding up. "The Absorption drones should do the rest. The media has also issued a press release asking that anyone feeling any signs of radiation sickness to contact their doctor immediately. If we get to it soon enough, everyone should be okay."

"At least everyone who wasn't killed by the blast," I reminded him.

"Yes," said the President sadly. "Except for them, of course. God rest their souls."

General Dalton looked up from a metered device in his hands. "This confirms it," he said. "It was definitely an Inferno bomb. Both the explosive and radiation patterns are identical."

I nodded, having assumed as much, and scanned the devastation below me again, wondering why I so badly felt the need to see it firsthand. Perhaps it was just a necessity for me to understand the enormity of what had happened. But, even with the intangible souls of over 3,000 innocent people below me, even with the unimaginable charred devastation, nothing seemed real. All this death. All this destruction. And for what? There was nothing ... *nothing* ... that could justify what had been done here today.

Maybe I hoped I could spot some kind of evidence. Any evidence. Bomb fragments. The ashen remains of the culprit. Blast patterns. Radiation signatures.

But another glance below and I knew all of that was fruitless. Sure, we'd been able to identify the explosive device and maybe there was a slim chance we could find a molecular piece of the bomber. But Inferno bombs are designed to leave nothing behind. Nothing but radioactivity and a singular blast pattern. All I had to do was look down to see how true that was.

So what the hell had driven me out here?

It came to me, settling over me like a warm blanket and feeling just as secure. I had to see the disaster for myself so that the fury within me would continue to burn. So that I wouldn't see it on the companel at home or in the MindFlicks or in NeuWorld and think of it as nothing more than a special effect or a tragic event separated from me by thousands of miles and 3,000 people I didn't know. So that my outrage at the senseless loss ... no, senseless *taking* ... of so many lives would never fade, would never shift, would never stop. At least until I had the son of a bitch responsible for this in the crosshairs of the flapjacker and I could pull the trigger, slamming him forever into a two-dimensional hell of his own.

Yes, as a veteran, the ZSW Memorial had meant something to me. But it was the lives destroyed today that haunted me the most. Those innocent, unsuspecting people who had come only to remember and to honor their loved ones. Those husbands and wives and sisters and brothers and daughters and sons and mothers and

34

fathers and aunts and uncles and grandmothers and grandfathers of those who had given everything they had to give to protect the civilization and the families they so loved. Wiped out by some madman or sick cult with a weapon that was so horrible it had been banned galaxy-wide a half dozen years before.

I realized my hands were shaking with pure, unadulterated rage. My lip had curled up in a snarl and a hot sweat had broken out over my forehead.

As though it were calling me, I could feel the flapjacker hanging beneath my coat and never in my life had I wanted a target so badly.

I was suddenly aware that the President and his associates were staring at me with something like fear on their faces.

Especially Hancock.

"Are you all right?" General Dalton finally asked. He raised his hand and rested it on my shoulder. "You look pale."

"Yeah," I lied, and took a deep breath. "I'm fine."

"Seen enough?" Hancock asked.

"Yeah," I said hoarsely. "Let's get the hell out of here."

The pilot pulled the Pod up and turned around, heading back for the White House. As our speed increased, the companel signal rang out and an image appeared on the windshield before us.

"Gentlemen," said the voice of the Secretary of Defense. "We have just received a message from what we believe to be a credible source claiming responsibility for the bombing."

We all exchanged grim but resolved stares.

"We're on our way," The President said, closing the communication. He turned to the Pilot.

"Double time," he ordered.

CHAPTER SIX

The deathly still in the war room was an almost tangible thing. The forty of us were there again, staring at the companel wall in the War Room awaiting the message we'd been told would be sent shortly.

Of course, it could be just another damned hoax. There'd been plenty of those already. What the hell was wrong with some people?

Hoax or not, at precisely the time promised, the companel lit up and the words "Audio Message Received" appeared there.

Boris snatched up a tiny remote control, pressed a button and waited. A moment later, a loud, tinny voice filled the room through a spatial speaker system.

"This is Burner," the message played, and I saw almost everybody in the room go rigid. "The bombing of the ZSW Memorial this morning was of my doing. Rest assured, there will be more incidents like this one. The Galactic Alliance has chosen to ignore the plight of the individual in exchange for a common government that feeds only the rich and exploits the poor. My organization will continue to fund, recruit and execute acts such as the event this morning until the Galactic Alliance acknowledges its errors and atrocities and the common man is put back into power. Do not bother to try and trace this message; it is impossible to do so. Heed my warning: Reverse the ways of the Galactic Alliance now or more innocents will die."

There was a burst of static and the audio went dead.

For a moment, there was complete silence.

"Burner could get his hands on an Inferno bomb," General Dalton stated. "Easily."

"Not these days," I said. "Burner's locked up in Kronos Asylum for the Criminally Insane. Been there for some time. This is either another frigging hoax or someone's trying to mislead us. Boris, did you try a trace?"

"And what would be the point of that?" Hancock asked impatiently. "The man clearly stated that a trace was impossible."

"Yeah," I spat back. "And Terrorists are best known for their truthfulness."

"We tried," Boris said glumly. "Nothing."

Hancock grunted smugly.

"Voice I.D.?" I asked Boris.

He shook his head. "Inconclusive."

"Interesting that he sent us an audio message and not full video," I said.

"Why?" asked the President.

"An audio message would be easier to record and smuggle out of Kronos than a full video clip."

"So maybe there's something to this."

"Maybe."

"I know who Burner is, of course. We all do," Janet Sutton said. "But he's not really someone we follow in the

38

Agricultural Department. What do we actually know about him?"

Solomon Pitt, the Special Services Commander, raised his hand. The President gratefully nodded.

Pitt took a deep breath. "Burner is a terrorist for hire. He works for anyone who pays him. We hunted him for nearly a decade before we bagged him two years ago at Valeria, seconds before he was going to assassinate a tribal priest. That assassination would have pitched Valeria into a bloody civil war that would have gone on for years, if not decades. He's taken credit for a number of smaller terrorist acts: a car bombing here, a kidnapping there. Small potatoes, really, especially when compared to what happened today."

"There are no small potatoes when it comes to terrorism," I said. "And Burner is directly responsible for more acts of terror than any other known terrorist."

The President nodded grimly as his assistant took furious notes. "What else?" he asked.

"Burner's strikes have always been quick and efficient and he's always gotten away clean, sir," said Pitt. "Until we took him on Valeria, that is." Pitt shook his head gently. "He's never attempted anything on a scale as large as what happened today, though. Not even close."

"Any connections to known groups?"

"He'll work for anyone who pays him."

"Anything else?"

"Well, there's his name," I said. "Burner's favorite

method of destruction is fire. He's done everything from throwing gasoline and matches on his targets to smaller Inferno technology attacks. Psychological profiles done on him after his capture indicate he's a pyromaniac ... as though we needed the psyche squad to tell us that. That diagnosis kept him out of a prison cell and put him in Kronos Asylum."

"So an Inferno bomb would be right up his alley," the President said.

"Right up his alley." I confirmed.

"But if he's locked up right now," Hancock asked, "How'd he do this?"

"I suppose it's possible that Burner masterminded something from Kronos," I said. "If he's really behind this, we've got to find out who hired him. Remember, he's always worked for the highest bidder." I turned my attention to Sonny Beach. "I think we should pay him a visit."

"The man is locked up in a high security mental hospital," Hancock grumbled. "This is a waste of time."

"It's our best lead so far," The President disagreed. "Mr. Fist, Mr. Beach. Go see what you can find out."

CHAPTER SEVEN

Sonny and I were in the Charger, heading to Kronos Asylum for the Criminally Insane at 6Flex speed. The diamond-bespeckled glory of deep space surrounded us. Outside, it was murderously cold. Inside the Charger, we were warm and toasty.

"Been a long time since we've been on a road trip," Sonny said. He took a long sip from the watercube he'd decompressed a few moments earlier.

"Probably since your bachelor party on *Pleasuria*," I replied, my lips curling into a smile at the memory. "Speaking of which, how are the wife and kids?"

"Fine, just fine," Sonny said. "Kids are growing up too damn fast and Embeth complains that you don't come by anymore."

I nodded. "I've been remiss. When this is all said and done, Candy and I will buy you guys dinner in Old San Diego."

"I'll hold you to that."

A chime sounded on the Charger's companel. We were being hailed. I touched the companel and the image of a man flashed onto the windshield before us. It was Chief of Security for Kronos Asylum, Jesse Crowe.

"Good morning, gentlemen," he said. "Thought I'd check in and see when I can expect you."

Crowe was probably in his early forties, younger than I would have expected from his deep, disciplinarian voice. He had a round but severe face, topped with a sprinkle of blondish-gray hair.

"We're about two hours out," I told him.

"Since we've got you on the line," Sonny said, "Tell us a little about Burner. Any problems with him lately?"

"None at all, Sheriff." He tapped away at a keyboard on his desk, read something on a virtual monitor there, and then looked back up at us. "Matter of fact, I'm looking at him from my office monitor right now. He's just lazing around."

"Has he had any unusual guests lately? Done anything differently?" I asked.

"No, not at all. First, he's not allowed any guests, for obvious reasons. As far as his behavior is concerned, he's been on his best for … oh, I don't know … the last month or so."

"What do you mean by that?"

"Well, sometimes the guy's a royal pain in the ass if you don't mind my saying so." I didn't. "Demanding certain foods, complaining about particular guards. The usual. But lately, he's been very obedient and calm. I think he's finally realized he's not getting out of here any time soon."

That raised a red flag. The phrase "calm before the storm" flashed through my mind. "Thanks, Mr. Crowe. We'll see you in a couple of hours or so."

"Great. Looking forward to meeting you face-to-face,

Mr. Fist. And it'll be good to see you again, Sonny."

"Same here, Jess. See you in a bit."

The image on the windshield blinked out.

"Sounds like Burner's been keeping a low profile," I told Sonny.

"Yeah. Like he doesn't want to draw any attention to himself ... because he's up to something."

"Maybe. We'll know in a few hours."

"Yes. That we will."

Kronos was the largest, criminal asylum in the galaxy. Built nearly a hundred years ago, the massive satellite looked like a planet-sized soccer ball made completely of iron armor. Its gray surface consisted of gigantic, interlocking panels and was symmetrically pocked by what looked to be giant rivets. There were no windows and only one entrance/exit - a thin, dark tunnel at the north pole of the sphere. Dozens of drone guards — if not hundreds - buzzed around the complex. Come too close without correctly answering their hail and they'd cut you to pieces in a matter of seconds. I'd seen the aftermath of several, wildly unsuccessful, escape attempts on the evening news. It wasn't a pretty sight.

As the Charger approached the narrow tunnel entrance, I answered the hail that was beamed to me with a unique clearance code - a series of numbers, letters and symbols that the President had personally given me before I left Earth. Still, the buzzing drones, now all pointed in my general direction, made me a little nervous. All that incredible firepower pointed at you will do that. Finally, when the windshield blinked a green approval code and the tractor beams from Kronos took us in their arms, a gentle wave of relief washed over me. Accepted code or not, the deadly aim of the drones never wavered.

As expected, the docking procedure was a number of increasingly tighter security checks but still took only a matter of minutes. The Kronos security team had their jobs down pat. They had to. In the case of a real emergency, there wouldn't be time to figure out how to do things right.

Uniformed guards armed with shatterguns met us at the dock and cordially escorted us to Jesse Crowe's office. They never uttered a word and not once did they let down their (you should excuse the pun) guard. After a short walk and a brief ride in a sterile white elevator, we were there.

"Gentlemen, please sit down," said Crowe, indicating a pair of wooden chairs that were placed in front of his dull, gray metal desk. In person, Crowe's hair was more blonde than it was gray. He held out a well-manicured hand, the back of which was speckled with fine white, almost transparent, hair. "I hope your trip was pleasant."

"Not bad," I told him, taking his hand and giving it a firm shake. "Just the same, I'm glad to finally be here. We don't have any time to waste."

"I understand." He touched the tip of his virtual monitor and the floating screen spun around to face Sonny and me. "Gentlemen, may I introduce you to Burner."

There, on the screen, stood the terrorist who called himself Burner. He didn't look so dangerous in his jail cell. He leaned his thin frame against the bars of his cell and stared into space. He appeared to be quite healthy and in fine physical condition. Obviously, he took advantage of whatever exercise program the prison offered. The yellow jumpsuit he wore appeared to be clean and new and the black shoes on his feet were shined to almost military perfection. His famous, naturally orange hair was perfectly coiffed, as though it had been freshly styled. His long face was clean shaven, his chin somewhat pointed. His nose was long and thin, like an arrow indicating the location of his mouth. He looked somehow suave, even in prison yellow. If it weren't for the jumpsuit, one might even think of Burner as a playboy type.

"As you can see, gentlemen, Burner is safe and sound and not going anywhere."

Staring at the image of Burner behind bars, I wondered if the message received at the White House was just another hoax after all. It was still possible that he had masterminded something from behind bars, but unlikely. You don't get a lot of unsupervised time at an Asylum for the Criminally Insane, especially if you're an intergalactic terrorist.

I stared at the image a moment longer, my mind lingering over the cell number painted just above the cell's sliding door. E-7. Something about it struck me but, for the moment, I couldn't put my finger on it.

"I assume you'll want to talk with him," Crowe was saying. "I've set up a room and we can have him transported there momentarily."

"Thanks, Jess," Sonny said. He started to stand.

"Just a minute," I said suddenly. Something had just sprung into my mind. "Warden, is your prisoner health schedule still in place?"

"Of course, Mr. Fist. We're required by law ..."

"I understand that. Now, tell me if I've got this right: prisoners are allowed showers every day, but full toiletries are on a once a week schedule, right?"

"That's right."

"And you still schedule those toiletries by cell block number."

"That's right."

"So when's the last time cell block E had their toiletries privilege?"

The Warden's eyes looked up as he calculated. "We have eight Cell Blocks set on a two month schedule. Cell Block A goes first, Cell Block B second, and so on."

"Yes, and when was Cell Block E last scheduled?"

Warden Crowe thought silently for a moment. "Four weeks ago," he finally said. "Actually, twenty-six days."

I took a deep breath.

I looked back to the monitor screen. Burner hadn't moved much. He'd gone from one side of the cell to the other but still leaned against the bars, hands at his sides, as though he were wishing for pockets.

"Okay," I said, moving closer to the picture and staring intently. "Now, is it just me, gentlemen, or does Mr. Burner here have too perfect a haircut for not having been groomed for nearly a month?"

Sonny looked closely, then said, "No. You're right. He looks freshly groomed."

"And I know some guys can't grow a beard," I continued, "But it's been four weeks and this guy doesn't even have a hint of stubble."

"Right again," Sonny said.

"Where are you going with this, Mr. Fist?" Crowe asked somewhat nervously.

"The bars on this particular cell, they're hooked into the main emergency system?" I asked.

"Of course they are."

"So they're riot-proofed, correct?"

A pause. Then: "Yes."

"The next time Burner touches those bars," I told him, "I need you to run a current of exactly 430 volts through them."

Crowe and Sonny stared at me with absolute silence.

"430 volts will kill him," Crowe said.

"I don't think so," I told him.

"Of course it will!" Sonny said.

"I don't think so," I repeated, more firmly. "Sonny, if I'm wrong here, I'll take full responsibility. You can charge me with murder, if you like. But we don't have time for games. Please back me on this."

Sonny stared at me with a combination of complete trust and confusion. "The President said you had his full authority," he said. He turned to Warden Crowe. "Do it, Jess."

Crowe hesitated. "I don't ..."

"Three thousand people may have been murdered by that man this morning," I reminded him.

"That's impossible, Mr. Fist. I told you, he hasn't been off prison grounds for two years." There was another, longer pause. "I'm sorry, Sonny. I can't do this on your authority alone."

"I understand," Sonny said. He reached into his coat pocket, withdrew his handcom, and quickly dialed a number. "Mr. President," he said after a moment, "Would you please confirm to Jesse Crowe that Mr. Fist has your full authority to do whatever he deems necessary regarding the bombing of the ZSW Memorial? Thank you, sir." He passed the phone to Crowe.

Crowe took the phone and began speaking.

I leaned closer to Sonny. "You have the President's direct line?" I whispered.

"He gave it to me before we left," Sonny told me. "For emergencies only."

"Of course," I replied.

Crowe was still speaking with the President. "You understand the risk here, sir ..." I could barely hear the buzz of the President's voice on the other end. Then,

Crowe said, "Very well, sir," and handed the phone to me. "He wants to speak with you."

I took the phone. "Mr. Fist," said the President, "I hope you know what you're doing."

"So do I, sir," I said. "Thank you."

I thought I knew what I was doing. I was 90% sure that I did. But that still left 10% room for a major league fuck-up. But there was no time for anything else.

I ended the connection and returned the handcom to Sonny.

"Ready when you are," Crowe told me.

I leaned closer to the monitor and waited. I locked my eyes on Burner's image, willing him closer to the metal grill. As if on command, he walked back and leaned against it, his fingers lacing around two bars, like a biker holding handlebars. "Now," I told Crowe.

"Sending," Crowe said. I heard the click of a switch but didn't take my eyes off the monitor.

On the screen, Burner suddenly jerked away from the bars as though shot. He stumbled and almost fell but managed to catch himself at the last moment. A tendril of blue smoke curled up from his burned palms. He straightened and stared at his fingertips, puzzled. His brows furrowed as his eyes went from his fingers, to the bars and back again.

And then he nodded and smiled wryly. He turned and stared directly at the prison camera.

At us.

Sonny and Crowe gave a collective gasp.

Because Burner's eyes had turned beet red, as though they were filled to bursting with hot blood.

And, occasionally, a blue spark shot out of one of them.

This wasn't Burner.

This wasn't even a human.

It was a goddamned android.

CHAPTER EIGHT

An android. A Burner android.

I hated androids. Despised them. This one was in particularly big trouble.

Sonny and Crowe sat in disbelief. "How did this happen?" Crowe asked.

"That's a good question," I told him. "And one that we have to answer. But right now, I need to interrogate that android."

"Yes, I understand," Crowe said. He took a sip of coffee. I could see that his hand was shaking. "Burner ... uh, the android ... can be transferred to an interrogation room as soon as you're ready."

"I'm ready now."

"Of course." Crowe pushed a button on his desk. He was still in a state of shock.

"Yes, sir?" answered a crisp voice from a speaker somewhere in the room.

"Transport prisoner 45467 to Interrogation Room 7A immediately, would you please?"

"Yes, sir."

"Give us a few minutes," Crowe said, "And we'll all go down together."

"Fine." I leaned back in my chair. "Now let's get back to your question: How did this happen?"

51

Crowe shook his head and I saw a cloud of anger and shame cross his features. "I don't have a clue," he said. "Of course, we'll be going over all of our records again, but we run a very tight ship here, Mr. Fist. We have to. All of our surveillance vidfiles are time-coded, veracity registered and double-checked just to be sure. There was no opportunity for someone to swap the real Burner with the android. Every entry and exit report is filed on time, accurately and completely. As you know, there are checks, double-checks and triple-checks to make sure that nothing is overlooked or can be faked. I've seen no evidence whatsoever that anything unusual took place here." He took another sip of coffee. "Our vidfiles are routinely examined by the security computer. No errors or omissions were reported. I'll put a team of experts on it now, but – in real-time – that could take weeks or even months."

"Or years," I grimly suggested. "We don't know when the swap took place. Could have been last week, last month or last year. Burner's been here two years, right? The exchange could have taken place at any time."

"I'm afraid so." Crowe rubbed his forehead wearily. "And even a real-time scan is no guarantee we'll find anything."

"What about medical records or routine checkups?" Sonny asked. "Wouldn't a full medical scan at least tell us when the real Burner was last examined? Give us a time table?"

Crowe shook his head. "Probably not. Modern android

technology is designed to fool even the most sophisticated medical equipment these days. Unless you're specifically verifying that someone isn't an android, you're not going to know. And, obviously, we had no inkling."

There was a pleasant beep from the desk and once again Crowe pushed a button. "Crowe," he said.

"Prisoner 45467 has been transferred, sir."

"Thank you." Crowe hit the button again and stood. "Shall we?"

♣

Interrogation Room 7A looked more like a surgery cathedral than an interrogation room. The walls rose up in a high-ceilinged dome and there was a ring of glass windows at the top. I could see chairs there where, at other times, onlookers could watch the proceedings. There was no one there now. The high level of security wouldn't allow it.

Sitting in the middle of the room, in a high-backed chair that could have come from a dentist's office (except for the supraplastic-enhanced straps designed to hold the "patient" in place) was the Burner android. The expression on its face feigned shock, surprise and outrage - a "what the hell am I doing here?" look.

I wasn't buying it for a minute.

While Crowe and Sonny took seats along the wall, I stepped up to the dentist chair and pulled a stainless steel tray there close to me. On the tray was a small wrench, a tiny screwdriver, a phase reducer, a laserblade, several stiff metal wires and a powerall switch. To the average human, it would have looked as though I were re-wiring the Charger. To an android, however, it would look entirely different.

It would look like pain.

"May I ask what this is all about?" the android asked indignantly. A chill ran down my spine but quickly fizzled as common sense set in. The voice was identical to the voice on the message we'd received that claimed credit for the ZSW bombing. Of course it was. The android had to be a perfect copy in order to pass itself off as the real Burner.

"You have the right," I replied. Then was silent.

After a moment, the android gave a nervous little giggle. It sounded real. "Well? What is this all about?"

"It's about the wanton destruction of three hundred city blocks. It's about the deaths of nearly 4,000 people. It's about the families that will never see them again. It's about the protection of freedom and the elimination of those who would try to snatch it away. It's about being human ... and that's something you're not."

The android cocked an artificial eyebrow at me. "If you expect me to deny that, don't waste your time," it said, surprising me with the admission. "You ran an electrical current of 430 volts through the bars of my cell, which ignited the phosphorous in my eyes. I was looking directly at a security camera at the time."

"Yes, you were," I told him. "But, if you hadn't been, we still would have registered the higher than normal heat signature around your eyes."

The android nodded, acquiescing. He jerked his chin toward the stainless steel tray beside me. "I don't know what you hope to accomplish with those. I was never programmed for pain. My application calls only for me to impersonate the human Burner with minimum bandwidth and highly restricted data storage."

"Maybe." I picked up the powerall from the tray and switched it on. A malignant brown/orange light ignited at its tip. "But that's what this is for. It's called a powerall, and its purpose is to upload all the programming you didn't originally receive – but that we now want you to have - in one quick jolt. If you really weren't programmed for pain, you will be when this is finished."

I leaned forward and snapped the Powerall against the android's ear. At first, I had a disturbing feeling as the hard metal of the Powerall wriggled against the lifelike flesh of the android's ear. That feeling faded after a moment as the Powerall locked into the artificial aural canal with a metallic click and the circuitry connection was completed.

The android's features never changed. He seemed neither concerned nor aloof. Completely emotionless.

That was all about to change.

A high-pitched chirp told me that the Powerall had completed the data transfer. I twisted it and removed it with a pop from the android's ear. I had another queasy moment when I saw that a tiny glop of fake ear wax stuck to the tip of the small machine.

I tossed the Powerall aside and gently touched the android's arm with my right hand. With my thumb and forefinger, I grabbed a big hunk of "flesh" and pinched, hard.

"Ouch! Shit!" the android screeched, and jerked his arm away violently. It wasn't much of a jerk thanks to the tight supraplastic straps holding him in place, but his eyes were suddenly full of genuine shock and dawning fear.

I smiled pleasantly. "Welcome to Pain," I said.

Then, I sorted through the tray, searching for the tool best suited for prying back cyborg fingernails.

Two hours later, Crowe and I were back at his office. My hands were numb from manipulating tiny instruments and my ears still rang with the fading screams of the Burner android. I sat back and rubbed my hands through my hair. My scalp was slick with sweat. I hated androids, but I hated torture even more. I tried to tell myself that the android wasn't human, that the pain it felt was artificial. It didn't make me feel any better about myself. I thanked God that this was something I didn't have to do often.

But I knew I'd do it again if I had to.

The door opened and Sonny entered with a tray of steaming coffee cups. He passed one to Crowe, one to me and took the last one for himself. As he settled back into a chair against the wall, Crowe looked up at me.

"So there was nothing?" he asked.

I took a sip of coffee, set the cup on the desk, and rubbed my eyes. I wasn't much of a coffee fan, but sometimes, you don't have a choice. "Well, he told us everything that was stored in his eye-mem banks," I said. By "eye-mem," I meant "I-Mem" or "immediate memory." Everything except his basic programming would be there – what he had for dinner each evening, what he watched on television, what he was told or what he overhead from his original programmers. The various methods of torture we'd just put the android through were designed to force the release of any information it had that it attempted to hide from us. It was all but impossible that it could have lied or withheld information - the pain we inflicted upon it was simply too great, especially when this was the first time it had ever experienced pain. Despite what you see in the Mindflicks or read in books, everyone has a breaking point. And, unlike humans, androids don't have the benefit of passing out when the pain becomes too great. I was convinced we had gleaned everything the android had to tell.

Unfortunately, it apparently knew nothing more than its immediate task: emulate Burner and convince the Warden and his subordinates that the real Burner was still in his cell.

"There's still secondary memory," Sonny reminded us.

"Yeah, but I don't hold out much hope there," I said. "This android was programmed so there's no need to use any secondary memory. Gives it a sort of 'plausible deniability.' The secondary memory is probably just blank."

Sonny bit his lip and sighed.

"Oh, we'll still check it," I continued. "I don't want to leave any stone unturned." I took a sip of my coffee and said to Crowe. "Where is the android now?"

"I asked that it be taken to infirmary immediately upon your completion of the re-set."

"Okay, we'll do the secondary memory flush there." I took another quick sip of coffee, grabbed my satchel off the floor and the three of us headed out the door.

It was a strange thing to see the android whom we had just tortured - who had been screaming and begging for his mommy (even though his mommy was nothing more than a supercomputer somewhere in the Jentillian system) - sitting up in bed, eating a fruit cup and chatting happily with a prison engineer. It was hard to imagine that anybody … or anything … could have gone through what the android had and even survive, much less scoop orange slices out of a plastic cup and remark on the beautiful weather.

The makeover had been my doing. After the interrogation was complete, I had wiped the android's immediate memory clean. I had squeezed every bit of information I could from its I-Mem and there was no reason to leave the memories of the torture session in the android's mind. It seemed unnecessarily cruel, even for an android.

58

I only wished I could wipe them from mine.

Crowe approached the engineer and asked him to give us a few moments. As he left the room, the Burner android looked up at us in puzzlement and then set his fruit cup on a nearby tray.

"Something I can help you with, gentlemen?" it asked.

"Actually, there is," I said. "My name is H.B. Fist, this is Jesse Crowe and this is Sheriff Sonny Beach." Crowe and Sonny nodded greetings. "We have reason to believe," I went on, "that adversaries of the Galactic Alliance have placed potentially dangerous material on your secondary memory. With your permission, I'd like to do a quick memory flush to see what's there."

The android looked up with something like fear in his eyes. I had wiped his memory clean but traces of his personality remained. "What exactly are you looking for?"

"We're not sure," I continued, "But we'll know when we find it."

"Will it hurt?"

"No. And it will only take a moment."

The android smiled. "Sure, then. Anything to help." It rolled over onto its stomach and pulled open the back of its hospital gown.

Ignoring the swell of nausea at the sight of android buttocks (there's something about them that doesn't ... I don't know ... look complete), I retrieved a small, square instrument from my satchel and activated it by pushing a flush switch on the side. It hummed to life. I lowered it to just above the android's waist and slid it gently up his spine, moving toward his neck until it locked into place, directly between his shoulder blades.

"Ow," the android said. "That's cold."

"Sorry," I said.

A moment later, another soft beep told me that the memory flush had been completed. I withdrew the instrument and glanced at the flashing red light thereon. "All done," I told him.

"That wasn't so bad," the android said, rolling over and sitting back up. "Was it any help?"

I looked at the face of the instrument. The tiny red light had changed to a tiny yellow one. I frowned.

"I'm afraid not," I said, my face registering disappointment, "But thanks for your time."

"You're welcome," the android said. He modestly closed his gown.

I shrugged at Crowe and Sonny and they followed me out of the room.

"Well, now what?" Sonny asked. "First the immediate memory was a bust. Now there's nothing on the secondary memory. Where do we go from here?"

"I never said the secondary memory was empty," I told him.

Crowe looked up sharply. "You told the android it wasn't any help."

"It may not have been." I held up the scanning device. The yellow light was now flashing green. "But there was *something* in the secondary memory. Until we download it into a mainframe, however, we won't know whether it's a take-out menu for a Chinese food restaurant or a photo résumé of our friend Burner."

"The mainframe in my office is fully secure." Crowe stepped up his pace in anticipation.

"Let's go see what we got," I said.

It took only a few moments to download the data that I had discovered in the secondary memory to the mainframe. Whatever it was, it wasn't much. Crowe's computer began to beep and twinkle as it swallowed the information and started to process it.

Just a few short seconds later, the computer announced it had completed its task. Crowe, Sonny and I gathered around the screen.

A tiny image appeared there, no bigger than an old-style postage stamp.

"Can't see anything," Sonny said.

"Magnify," Crowe ordered. The computer zoomed in on the image. It was nothing but a multi-colored blur now.

"Enhance," Crowe said.

The image seemed to fold in on itself but, in a moment, began to take shape. Finally, we could see detail.

"It's a map," Sonny said.

"Part of one, at least," I added. "Looks like it was torn out of a book, or something." I pointed to the roughness of its edges.

"It's certainly not hand-drawn." Crowe pointed to the

61

screen. "Pixels. This was printed commercially."

I smiled. "Then we should be able to find it. May I use your companel?" Crowe nodded and I stepped over and sat down at his desk. In a few seconds, I had dialed Boris Cushing's personal number on Earth and his image was floating a few feet away from me.

"Boris, I need you to run a piece of data for me."

"Anything you need, H.B."

"Sending it to you now." I nodded and Crowe hit a button on his mainframe. We waited while Boris checked his companel and gave me an okay sign with his sausage-like fingers.

"I've got it," he said. "What do you need to know?"

"We need to know where that piece fits," I told him. "It's part of what seems to be a commercially printed map. See if you can find which one."

"If it was printed anywhere in the Alliance," Boris said, "We'll find it. Give me a few minutes."

I sat back and put my hands behind my head.

Waiting. The hardest part.

Crowe pulled out a cigarette and offered me one. I declined. He turned to Sonny, who also shook his head.

"Got any Reyes?" Sonny asked.

Crowe nodded. "Right hand drawer."

I slid it open, grabbed the bottle and three of the four shot glasses therein, and set them on the table. Crowe poured three generous shots. "*Salud.*"

We drank.

A moment later, Boris's voice returned. "Gentlemen, we've got a match."

"Tell me."

"It was published two years ago by O. Atlas Cartographers in Beverly Hills, CA. That particular map is of *Arbol de Hoja Perenne*, the Evergreen Planet, in the Novya sector."

I pushed myself away from Crowe's desk and stepped to his computer. Keying "*Arbol de Hoja Perenne*" onto the keyboard there, I found an encyclopedia entry. According to the entry, the "Evergreen Planet" was lush, verdant, uninhabited, and out of the way of any commercial spaceship routes.

In other words: A perfect place to hide. Especially if you were a terrorist as well known and as universally hated as Burner.

"Boris," I said. "Tell the President we may have something. We're on our way home."

CHAPTER NINE

The setting sun bathed the homes on the hills that overlook the city of Ventura, California with a warm, golden hue. Soaking in the fading warmth of the day's last light, I brought the Charger closer to home.

As I drew nearer, I could see our home. It jutted up from the rounded hill like a huge beige shoebox (a shoebox in the old adobe style, of course), and seemed to sit precariously, hanging onto the graded cliffside for dear life. Friends have told me that – during the next big earthquake – my home is going to roll down the hill and onto the houses below it. Me, I figure whatever will be will be. Anyway, with California now resting on seismic shock absorbers, I wasn't too worried about it.

The lights were on in the kitchen and I could see a shadowed figure moving about inside. Candy was already home. I saw the shadow kneel and knew she was putting a bowl on the floor, feeding Sonova.

The maw of the garage door yawned open and the onboard navcom gently guided the Charger in for a picture perfect landing. I sat there in the garage for a moment, feeling a tiny piece of the long day's tension fade away. That relaxation wouldn't last long. I was home long enough just to make a couple of calls, pack my bags and have a brief dinner with my wife. Then it was back to D.C.

to discuss what we'd discovered at Kronos.

I stepped out of the Charger, told the computer to close the garage roof, and entered the kitchen. The scent of Candy's trademark homemade enchiladas crept into my nostrils and my mouth watered in anticipation. I shrugged out of my leather duster and hung it on the hook by the door.

Sonova saw me first, of course, and gave a happy little yipe. Then, his feet flailing on the slick tile floor like a character in a Warner Bros. cartoon, he skittered across the room to me where he jumped up and happily nipped at my hands. Finally, I had to put my face down where he could give it a quick lick or two. Satisfied, he went back to his bowl of gravy-drenched meat lumps, of which my cheeks now reeked.

I watched him happily scarf down his dinner and envied his canine naïveté.

Candy stepped over, her eyes still showing signs of sadness and stress from yesterday's bombing, and put her arms around me. We held each other for a few healing moments and all was silent. All, that is, except for the liquid lapping of Sonova and his dinner.

Candy finally released me and went back to the stove. She picked up a ladle and stirred red enchilada sauce. "Rough week," she managed. Her voice was a little raspy.

"Yeah. Pretty rough," I replied. I took another whiff of the delicious air. "Mmm. Enchiladas."

Candy smiled a little. "Enchiladas. They sent us all

home early again today because ... because they feared more attacks. I guess everybody and everything's a target again. They don't want us back for at least a couple of days so I'm telecommuting. I thought I'd take advantage of the extra time and cook you your favorite meal." She looked thoughtful for a moment. "I had a feeling you won't be home for long."

I nodded. Then, as she put the final touches on the meal, I told her everything that had happened that day. I wasn't worried about loose lips sinking any ships – Candy's Top Secret clearance was higher than my own.

A few moments later she slid a plate with two luscious enchiladas, a dollop of rice and a splash of refried beans on a plate before me. Finely grated cheese was sprinkled across the entire plate. Mine had a glob of sour cream on top of each enchilada; Candy's did not.

I wondered, briefly - and not for the first time - why they called them refried beans. Did they fry them twice? I didn't know. Then again, I didn't really care. They were delicious and that's all that mattered.

"So if Burner's not at Kronos," Candy asked, sitting down at her place at the table, "Where is he?"

"That's the big question." I shoved a forkful of enchilada into my mouth and chewed. The combination of tortilla, cheese, sauce and sour cream was wonderful. "I'd bet my left foot that he wasn't on Earth when the bombing took place. It'd have been all but impossible for him to get past security. He's too well known and well-recorded. And, like most top level terrorists, he's too much of a pussy to do his own bidding." I chewed quietly for a moment, relishing the savory flavor. "That only leaves the rest of the galaxy for him to hide out in."

"What if he used a falseface to get past scanners?"

"He would have had to use a falseface and someone else's body. His DNA is on file in the Earthshield. If he tried to get in, we would have been notified. If he even gets close, we'd know."

"So it's impossible."

"Well ... nothing's impossible."

"Any ideas?"

I shook my head. "Nope. Not one. Burner's a psycho bastard but he's not stupid. It won't be easy to find him."

I sipped a bit of the margarita that Candy had served me and smiled with delight. It was perfect. She still made the best margaritas in the galaxy and I've sampled them everywhere.

Candy quietly mixed a spoonful of beans and rice. She looked up at me with a sad, concerned expression. "Will there be another attack?"

I nodded grimly. "Unfortunately, it's pretty likely," I said. "That's what makes this so urgent. We've got to find this bastard before that can happen."

Candy put the fork into her mouth and chewed slowly and without pleasure. The skin on her face looked like paper for a moment - fragile and gray. Her eyes looked into the distance at a future that suddenly wasn't so certain.

BURNER

I stared at her and another surge of rage swelled in my chest. I forced it back into its cubbyhole - I'd need it later - but right now I needed to comfort my wife. I put my hand out and covered hers. "I'll get him, Candy. I promise."

Candy's forced smile faltered. "I know you will, H.B.," she said. "I just hope you get him soon ..." She took a tiny sip of her maggie and I saw raw anger boil behind her eyes. I recognized it as the junior partner to my own. "... and I hope you get him good," she finished.

We finished our dinner in contemplative silence.

Later, after I had packed my overnight case, minimized it with the flapjacker and tucked it behind the seat of the Charger, I stepped back into the kitchen. Candy was sitting at the dining table, a glass of Valley of the Moon Chardonnay 2065 in her hand. I could see the worry clearly on her face but I saw something else there, too: grim determination. I stepped up behind her and put my arms around her, nuzzling my face gently into her hair.

She reached up and took my hand. "Be careful, H.B."

"I will. You know that."

"I know."

I gave her a quick kiss and stepped into the living room. The companel was alight with messages; I'd download them to the Charger and read them along the way. But I had one important call to make before I left. I punched up the call screen and entered a number.

The companel lit up before me and indicated that the line was ringing. A moment later, the image of a Spartan living room appeared there. All I could see was a sofa, a coffee table and an end table on which was a purple lava lamp, sexily oozing. None of the items were particularly decorative.

A man sat on the sofa, staring back at me. He was wearing fatigues and his pockets were loaded with what were probably deadly weapons of intense pain and total destruction. His feet were encased in battle boots - soft, light protective leather that was nearly as strong as armor. I recognized them instantly as standard issue from my time in the ZSW. A duffel bag sat beside the man, packed to the gills with God only knew what.

The man's expression was tight and determined. I could see yet another facsimile of the rage that burned within me reflected in his eyes.

"I wondered when the fuck you were gonna call me, boy," growled Sergeant Bruno, grabbing at his duffel bag and standing. "I assume you're on your way to pick me up?"

CHAPTER TEN

I was back in the war room with nearly forty world leaders, military commanders and, of course, Boris Cushing. Sgt. Bruno stood beside me. He hated being here with the people who made the decisions. He was a warrior, a man of action. He wanted to get going, now, not later. I could feel his impatience boiling from where I stood.

The din of raised, angry voices filled the air like so many fingernails on so many chalkboards. I sat with my head in my hands, enduring the unbelievable bullshit rhetoric and maintaining my composure by the slimmest of margins.

But I knew it wouldn't hold forever.

"We've got to go in and crush them now," screamed Presidential Advisor Colin Hancock. "For all we know, they're already planning another strike." He pounded his fist on the table for emphasis.

"Isn't there a way to contact them?" someone else said. "Talk to them? Find out what their grievances are?"

"This has to be handled diplomatically ..."

"An airstrike is the only way to be sure ..."

I rolled my eyes in disgust and glanced over at Boris. His massive, exhausted body leaned against his glistening support machinery, a sad, helpless look on his face. After a moment, he looked at me and we shook our heads in disappointed unison.

"Surely, violence isn't the only answer ..."

"Blacken the entire planet. Send a message to them all ..."

Vaguely, I heard a pounding noise coming from the other end of the room. At first, it was almost inaudible over the rising din but it continued, growing louder and more urgent with each beat. Soon, it became a powerful slamming like a sledgehammer against a wall. The desks around me shook from the impact.

It was the President. He was banging what was left of his coffee cup on the desktop. Bits of porcelain were scattered on the floor in front of him and broken chunks of cup littered his desk and the desks nearby him. I could see a widening brown stain being absorbed by probably Top Secret documents.

The din died down almost instantly.

The President took a deep, angry breath and glared, red-eyed, at the entire room. "Pardon me for interrupting," he finally growled. "But we don't have time for this pointless bickering."

Those who had been doing the bickering exchanged final dirty looks and then took their seats quietly, giving the President his berth.

"I need to make a decision," the President continued. "And in order to make that decision, I need information." A number of hands immediately shot up, demanding attention, but the President ignored them. "I don't want to hear any extremist nonsense. We are not going to nuke an entire hemisphere of another world nor are we going to sit back on our hands and gently ask someone to explain themselves. I want some constructive suggestions and I want them now."

Hancock stood. "Mr. President," he said, his voice a study in calm. "I understand your desire for restraint. But we can't wait on this. We've got to hit them hard now. The longer we delay, the better the chance they move their base of operations."

"We don't know that this is their base of operations ..."

"Mr. Fist simply found a map ..."

"It doesn't mean that this is where they're hiding ..."

"We just can't go in like cowboys, guns blazing..."

And they were off to the races again. Yelling. Screaming. Pumping fists. Pointing fingers.

The President looked around the room in stunned disbelief. He raised his coffee cup again and discovered he now held only the handle. Reaching over to the person beside him, he grabbed their coffee cup and began banging it, almost instantly shattering it into pieces.

The room quieted a lot faster this time. Everyone looked at the President with a combination of anger and shame.

"I asked for information and suggestions," he said after a moment. "I want no more screaming. I want no more arguing. I want to make a decision based on facts."

The room remained silent. No one wanted to be the

first voice in what was sure to be a new cacophony.

So I stepped in.

"Mr. President, I have a recommendation."

The President nodded in my direction. "Go ahead, Mr. Fist."

"Sir, I would recommend sending maybe a dozen platoons of Marine Devilbats to *Arbol de Hoja Perenne.* Three of those platoons can hit the ground ..."

"Three?! Only *three?*" Hancock screamed in furious disbelief. "You'd be signing their death warrants!"

Several loud voices cried out again, challenging or cheering the Presidential advisor. They were instantly silenced when the President smashed his cup on the table again, sending more white fragments ricocheting through the air.

When calm was restored once again, the President turned his attention back to me. "Please continue, Mr. Fist. You won't be interrupted again." He glared around the room, making it clear that his word was golden.

"As I was saying, sir, send a dozen platoons of Marine Devilbats to *Arbol de Hoja Perenne* and keep nine of them in orbit, out of sight, in a state of high readiness. While they're orbiting, three advance teams can canvass the area and see who and what the hell is really down there."

"And if the advance teams are captured or killed?" Hancock spat.

"Then the nine remaining combat teams will be ready to move in."

"And if the intel reports prove wrong and there's nothing there?" someone else asked.

"Then we'll turn around and come home. Time wasted but no harm done."

The President considered my comments for a moment and then asked, "Any objections?"

A half dozen hands went up, including Hancock's. The President ignored them.

"Do it," he told me. "General Dalton, make it happen."

I nodded my gratitude and the President dropped the remnants of his second coffee cup on the table in front of him. As he exited the war room, I noticed Colin Hancock staring in my direction.

He touched two fingers to just below his eyes and then pointed directly at me. It was the stale "I'm watching you" cliché.

I touched two fingers to my eyes, too ... and then pointed back with an entirely different finger. Before Hancock could respond, I turned and walked away.

CHAPTER ELEVEN

It was as cold as space in the troop transport ship, and space is pretty fucking cold.

Our vessel and two others exactly like her sliced through the upper atmosphere of *Arbol de Hoja Perenne* like a behemoth great white shark through dark water. Our vessel was the lead ship, containing the Alpha Team; the other two contained the Beta and Gamma Teams. All were ready for battle, if it came to that.

And I had a sad hunch it would come to that.

We were on course toward *Vendarje*, the most highly vegetated area of *Arbol de Hoja Perenne*, an enormous jungle that carpeted about a quarter of this hemisphere. According to our advance drones and orbital scans, a large number of enemy troops had set up camp there, and were keeping their heat, light and sound signatures damped. In other words, they were trying to stay hidden. Because the jungle greenery was so thick - impenetrable with our eyes in the sky and too dangerous for our drones to navigate – we had to rely on magnetometers and radiation detectors to gauge the terrorists' weapon cache. Based on that information, the planet below had stores of everything from handguns and grenades to missiles, small battlespheres and more. Exactly the kind of weapons necessary for waging a surprise war on an unsuspecting

75

world.

Interestingly, there was no sign of gunspore.

We sat in silence, breathing shallowly, making the most of the thin air. Layers of foil blankets were clutched around us, trapping our natural body heat and keeping the temperature tolerable, if not comfortable.

Talking was strictly forbidden (it was too cold to talk, anyway) and even the oxygen generators were set for minimum circulation. The audio signature of both idle chatter and spinning ventilation fans can be recognized by sophisticated detection equipment, and we wanted our visit to be an unwelcome surprise.

Those aboard the transport were well aware of their orders and they had come prepared. They sat stoically, ignoring the cold, and waited for the signal that it was time to go to war. Their faces were masks of grim determination.

I briefly took inventory of the Marine Devilbats around me. They all wore full battle armor, the dull black shielding giving them a passing resemblance to the knights of old. They were King Arthur's Round Table with shatterguns and bamzookas instead of swords and lances. The look on each of their faces said that killing wasn't necessarily their favorite way of settling things but today, they were ready, willing and able. They had spent most of their lives training to be ready for action when duty called and, when the ZSW Memorial had been erased with a huge blue flame, that call had come loud and clear.

My armor wasn't quite as heavy as the Marines was. I'd been a civilian too long and wasn't up to wearing the heavy stuff. I was in fairly good shape but I was no Devilbat. The armor I wore was police issue, not Marine issue. It would stop small arms fire but a shattergun blast would probably cut me in two.

I still felt pretty safe knowing that I'd have a platoon of full-blown Devilbats at my side.

Not to mention Sgt. Bruno.

The shattergun slung over my shoulder gave me a strange sense of déjà vu, even though it'd been nearly six years since I carried one in the ZSW. I'd left the flapjacker far behind on this trip. It was securely locked up in the Charger, which itself was parked back at the Port Hueneme Naval Base in California. The flapjacker was a personal weapon, not a weapon of war. If we were going into battle on the planet surface below, I wanted as much destructive force as possible at my beck and call. The flapjacker was cruel and efficient but a shattergun would blow a man and his neighbor into a hundred meaty chunks.

Sgt. Bruno sat beside me, his face a master's study of stoicism. He, too, had rejected the offer of modern Marine armor and instead wore his old ZSW proteksuit. It was a stripped down version of what the Devilbats were wearing, boasted a dark camouflage pattern and wore scorches and bullet nicks like medals. Fashion-wise, Bruno stood out like the proverbial sore thumb, but he was probably as well-protected as any of the Devilbats. Those old proteksuits were made to last.

Still, occasionally I saw one of the younger Marines look over at Bruno and give a little smile, probably thinking how cute the old man looked in his antique war uniform. I thought it was a good thing Bruno was ignoring everyone, or he might decide to show them how "cute" he really was – and wind up dangling a Devilbat out of a hatch by his boot straps.

I sat back and rested my head against the cold metal wall. It thrummed sweetly with the throb of the engines running in silent mode as we bore our way into the heart of *Arbol de Hoja Perenne*.

Bruno reached into one of his utility pockets and withdrew a small tin canister. He pried it open, exposing an orange-ish paste inside. With the tip of his little finger, he scooped a tiny glop about the size of a pea out of the tin and rubbed the paste inside of his gums, both top and bottom. His eyes closed in apparent pleasure as he savored the flavor of whatever the hell that was.

"Didn't know you were one for snuff," I whispered.

"Ain't snuff," he said quietly. "You never heard of Stathe?"

"Stathe?"

"Yeah, Stathe. Statham 666. It's a battle performance enhancer. Focuses the mind, adds a little strength to the muscles. Makes you more aware of your surroundings and gives you an added edge in reaction time."

"Does it work?"

"Always worked for me."

"So that little glop does all that?"

"That little glop is all you ever want to take. Any more than that ... well, I've seen guys go crazy. Kill everything in their way and then stroke out or their heart bursts. It ain't pretty."

He passed me the tin. "Wanna give it a try?"

"I'll pass," I said. "Isn't that stuff illegal?"

"The best things always are," Bruno said. He passed the tin to the marine next to him and watched as he, too, took a tiny pinch and passed it on.

A few moments later, a red bar lit up along the sides of the transport and we all looked up in unison. We were getting close; it was time to head for our designated HALU drop tube. There was no need for discussion – we had all done HALU drops dozens of times before, either in actual battle situations or in intense simulations. Three single file lines were formed, each leading toward one of three drop tubes near the tail end of the transport. I felt a tug as someone checked my lunar umbrella pack. It was latched tight. I returned the favor and confirmed theirs was operational, too. We were still running silent so a hand on the shoulder was all the confirmation we could give.

The first Devilbat entered the drop tube and slid the glass door closed behind him. He fixed his mask over the lower half of his face and gave a hearty thumbs up. A moment later, the red light on the tube flashed to yellow, then quickly to green. The floor dropped out and the marine vanished into the night. It took less than a second for the tube to re-pressurize and then the next marine stepped in. The process was quickly repeated.

And so, like lemmings into the sea, we entered the drop tubes one-by-one and were expelled from the transport ship toward the planet below.

HALU (or High Altitude Lunar Umbrella) dropping isn't a lot of fun. You're at high altitude, so it's too cold; you don't use your lunar umbrella until the last moment so it's too fast and - because you most often drop at night - it's too dark. Unfortunately, it's also the most clandestine way to infiltrate enemy lines without being shot into a billion pieces before you hit ground. I'd rather be uncomfortable than dead.

As I began the 25,000 foot drop toward the planet below, I found myself wishing I simply could have tele-transported. But a tele-transportation beam can sometimes be seen by the naked eye and is simple to detect with the right equipment. Without a doubt, HALU dropping was the best way to go, at least in this situation.

After several minutes of free-falling, I felt the lunar umbrella spring open from my backpack. I braced myself for the ensuing violent tug. As expected, the umbrella, energized by the gravitational pull of the planet's several moons, grabbed tight onto the night air and gave me a solid yank, slowing my fall to a safe speed as I neared the planet surface. I activated my optic scanner and searched for the electronic signature of others below. They were close. Our automated guidance systems had put us almost on top of each other.

I hit the ground, rolled to avoid being wrapped up in the now flaccid lunar umbrella behind me and crouched down, darting my eyes in every direction. A thick, black jungle surrounded me - ropy vines and mammoth tree trunks, all tightly woven together by Mother Nature. It would take some serious maneuvering and a machete or torch to pass through.

A tap on my shoulder sent a quick jolt through me and I whirled to find myself face-to-face with Bruno.

"All right?" he whispered.

"All right," I replied.

A number of shadows began to materialize from the bushes around us. The Devilbats. They surrounded us like a metal cocoon and awaited orders.

Commander Robert Stimson, a tall marine with a huge push-broom mustache, approached us. "How far are we from the target?" he asked in a hushed tone.

"About a mile," answered one of the Marines.

"This ain't gonna be easy," Bruno said. He nodded, indicating the thick, winding brush surrounding us.

"Yeah," Stimson said. "This vegetation is much thicker than we anticipated."

"Can't hack through it," I added. "Even with all of us working at it, it'd take forever to cut through with machetes. I think we have to go with the lasertorches."

"We do that," Stimson said, "And we risk exposing our

location with firelight."

"What if we wait until daylight and then burn our way through?" Bruno asked.

"Still no good," Stimson replied. "Ever hear of smoke signals?"

Bruno nodded and mused for a moment. "Screw it, then. Let's burn through now. We'd better save our strength in case we're engaged and, anyway, this vegetation might be so dense that no one will notice the light."

Stimson considered. "I don't think we have any choice." He turned toward a nearby Marine with a mini-navcom. "Which direction?"

Without missing a beat, the Marine pointed and said, "This way."

Stimson waved his arm over his head and the Devilbats fell obediently into place behind him.

We walked as far as we could before the vegetation became too thick to pass through. It wasn't very far. Stimson ordered a couple of Devilbats up front and they activated the cutting torch. It sparked to life with a blue-white hotness that left a jagged image in my eyes long after the Marine had tuned it to the less obvious blue. They began cutting.

The jungle vines were as tightly interwoven as fibers in a carpet. Our cutting progress ground to a crawl. "At this rate, we won't be there 'til dawn," I grumbled.

"That'll work," Stimson replied. "We'll have the chance to do some close-up reconnoiter and get a little rest. We'll move on the enemy camp at dusk."

I turned to watch the Marines at work and again worried about the unavoidable delay. The longer it took us, the more likely we would be spotted. Standing together in one place while we waited for someone to clear a path wasn't a good place to be.

As if to prove that point, a leaf beside my left ear suddenly vaporized in a blast of white hot light and Bruno started shouting, "Down, down, down!" I dropped to the ground and freed my shattergun from its restraints.

We were under fire. Snipeblazers.

I rolled behind the nearest hard cover - a small boulder buried beneath vines and leaves - and tried to get a handle on the situation. Peering cautiously over the rock into the clearing behind me, I could just make out a couple of untidy lumps in the darkness there. They were two Marines, already down, huge steaming death holes puckering their uniforms where the armor had failed.

More fire flashed around me. I ducked, feeling the warmth as another beam of heat flashed over my head. I peeked out from behind my rock again and watched as more fire exploded from an area at my eleven o'clock position. Although I could see nothing but black on darker shades of black, I knew that at least one of the snipers firing on us was hidden there. Using the rock as a brace, I aimed the shattergun and pulled the trigger three times in quick succession.

The black area in front of me lit up and - for a fleeting

second - I could see the sniper's shocked face as the shattergun blasts hit him. Then, all I could see was a spray of dark ribbons and grey chunks and the laserfire stopped.

There were a few moments of silence, deafening in the wake of all that gunfire. Slowly, someone nearby stood up. The silhouette of a huge mustache told me it was Stimson. He held his hands in the cease fire position as he cautiously surveyed the area, his eyes completely circling the clearing to make sure he missed nothing. After a moment, he began to lower his arm to give the all clear ...

... and his hand disappeared in a yellowish-red haze of flesh and fire. A split second later, his body jerked as more laserblasts cut through it. His lifeless form collapsed to the damp earth.

I had only a vague idea of where the second sniper was hiding but didn't have a direct line of fire from my current position. I squinted over the rock and was rewarded with a blast of tiny particles as another shot ricocheted off the stone in front of me. A streak of rock glowed orange-red for a moment and then faded away as it cooled. I dropped to my belly and traced the edge of the rock along the ground, peering from behind as I came to the outer edge. No use. I still had no sightline to the second sniper's location.

Another shot blasted from the sniper's position and then suddenly went wild - firing directly up into the sky - and I heard a gurgling gag that started as a scream and died as a choking gasp. There were another few moments of intense, hanging silence and then Sgt. Bruno stepped into the clearing, holding a thin piece of razor wire between his fingers and cleaning it with his thumb and forefinger. He hacked up a monster of a loogy and spat it on the ground. I noticed that his ZSW armor was freshly blackened and pitted in several places - but not burned through.

"Olly Olly Oxen," Bruno called casually, slipping the razorwire back into the hollows of his fake finger. After a few moments, several Devilbats crawled out from their hiding places, brushing dead leaves and soil from their armor. I got to my feet and stepped closer to Bruno.

"We lost Stimson," I said.

"Yeah," Bruno said simply, spitting again.

I surveyed the carnage around me. "Those snipeblazers burned right through that Marine armor. Good thing you wore your old stuff."

Bruno slapped it proudly. "Kept me alive then and kept me alive now. You can keep this fancy-shmancy new stuff. Won't keep the goddam ants out, much less a snipeblazer beam."

"They know we're here now," I said.

"Doesn't matter," Bruno continued. "They only know where *we* are. Beta and Gamma Teams have been on the ground for some time now and I don't see or hear any other signs of battle." Bruno took a deep breath and smiled with grim satisfaction. He cocked his shattergun. "Damn, I miss killin' bad guys," he said. "Let's go find us some more."

85

CHAPTER TWELVE

Our nearly depleted group, which had started out as twenty-five but was now cut down to eight, had lost any element of surprise we might once have had. The short but deadly gunfight that had served as our welcome wagon was absolute evidence of that. The best thing that could happen now was that the remaining terrorists would flood to our position to engage us. Then, the other two Devilbat teams could swing in from behind and clean house. That didn't bode well for what was left of Alpha Team, but that's the way war works.

Commander Stimson's death left us without a commanding officer so Bruno stepped in easy as you please to take over. Despite the fact he'd been retired for a number of years, he outranked everybody still standing and the younger troops – now a little less invincible after the devastating snipeblazer attack – were only too happy to accept him and his veteran expertise.

"One thing's certain - they know we're here," Bruno told us as we edged closer to the terrorist camps. "That means they'll either send another greeting party or that they'll close up shop nice and tight so they can prepare for our arrival. Either way, it works for the other teams. If they come for us, that means fewer bad guys in the camp and fewer to put up a fight when Beta and Gamma arrive. If they lock up camp, they'll expect an attack from our position, not the others'. The bottom line here is that we've got to keep moving quickly toward the target. If we're lucky, we'll bump into their troops on our way in and surprise the hell out of them."

Bruno tapped the headset he had relinquished from Stimson's body and cocked his head, listening carefully. "Still nothing from the others," he said. "I gotta believe the enemy are jamming the frequency."

"More evidence they know we're here," I noted.

"Yep," Bruno said. "But sometimes knowing ain't enough. And this is one of those times."

We crept through the bushes, keeping our eyes and ears open for any sign of the enemy. Since the initial ambush, there had been nothing. No attacks, no surprises, no bodies. Nothing. It was almost eerie.

Finally, after about three hours of intense cutting and slow marching, the jungle seemed to ease up a bit. It certainly wasn't the yellow brick road, but the going got a lot easier. Before long, we climbed over an ivy-laden hill overlooking a deep and vast valley. Bruno stopped suddenly.

Spread out below us was the terrorist camp our drones had spotted earlier. There were perhaps a hundred small tents – individual homes – and a couple of large communal ones – probably showers and mess halls. Watchtowers sat neatly in each corner. A few fires danced merrily near the center of the makeshift village. The blue hue of the moons gave everything a cool, calm look that spoke of peace, not war.

And it was very, very quiet.

"Where is everyone?" a Marine asked behind me.

"It's four in the morning," I whispered. "Everybody's in bed."

Bruno shook his head. "No, he has a point. Even if everyone's in bed, there'd be *somebody* up and moving. Guards, cooks, the milkman. Something's not right."

A tiny movement caught my eye and I squinted, pinpointing the source. I reached out and gave Bruno's sleeve a little tug. He looked in the direction my finger pointed, raised his eyebrows, and nodded worriedly.

"Humonkeys," he whispered.

There, near one of the tents, was a humonkey tied to a post. A bowl half full of dried chow buzzed with flies by its side. The humonkey slept soundlessly, its chest rising and falling with each breath. Occasionally, its furry feet twitched as it dreamed of a life of freedom back in the jungle.

Once we located that first humonkey, the others were easy to find. There were dozens of them tied up throughout the campsite, each with its own bowl, most sound asleep.

"What is this? A zoo?" asked a confused Marine.

Apparently, he had forgotten his high school biology lesson: *Which animal's biological signature is nearly impossible to differentiate from that of a human being?* The answer was: A humonkey - a species of monkey that called the very deepest parts of Africa its home. It hadn't even been discovered until just some thirty odd years ago.

"It's not a zoo," Bruno told the Marine. "It's a trap."

On cue, the brush around us suddenly belched out what appeared to be about a dozen heavily armed monks. They wore robes printed in dark camouflage colors that couldn't be detected in the jungle night and hoods were pulled down over their faces so that only an inky black oval was visible. They surrounded us silently, jerking hellishly huge rifles in our direction and making it painfully clear we were to drop our weapons or they would blow us to pieces where we stood.

We had no choice. The only way out was suicide and we weren't ready for that.

Not yet.

"Put your weapons down and do as they say," Bruno ordered.

"But, Sarge," one of the younger Marines said, "They aren't *saying* anything."

Bruno gave him an exacerbated glance. "You know what I mean, Monzon. Now, do it."

With a rough nudge of their weapons, the dark monks led us away from the decoy camp and back into the jungle.

We marched for the better part of an hour until the monks stopped us in front of a rock wall, surprisingly devoid of any vegetation. Most of them held us in position with pointed weapons while three approached the wall.

Each removed a small handheld device from within their robe, activated a series of commands on its small screen, and then waited.

A few seconds later, the stone wall flickered before us and I realized it wasn't a real wall at all. It was something like a falseface, a hologram, an illusion. Where the wall once was now yawned the entrance to a manmade tunnel leading down into the ground.

Pointing the way with their shatterguns, the monks forced us inside. As we marched deeper, the glowing dawn of the new day slowly faded to black behind us.

CHAPTER THIRTEEN

Some of the greener marines were grumbling under their breath behind us. They wondered why Sergeant Bruno had surrendered so easily instead of putting up a fight. But I knew what he was thinking: A dead soldier can't finish the job. Once you're dead, your options for completing a mission diminish ... well, considerably. By staying alive, even if you're captured, the possibility of completing your mission still exists. Bruno was hoping that our underground excursion would keep the attention focused on Alpha Team, giving the other teams a chance to get the job done before being detected.

A series of flickering torches guided our way as we went deeper and deeper into the tunnel. The air grew colder and damper around us. Grimly, I realized that the deeper we went, our chances of success and escape diminished.

The monks marched us on for about twenty minutes or so and then brought us to another halt in a small stone anteroom. There were more torches here so I took the opportunity to try and get a better look at them. I could still only see shadows for faces but, beneath their monk-like robes, our captors were apparently wearing fairly modern armor and matching uniforms, not the ragtag mish-mash I would have expected from a terrorist military. In addition, each man also carried an identical weapon - what looked like a WarMaker 1500 multi-phase unit, a combination snipeblazer and assault rifle. That explained the blistering holes in our dead Marines' armor, but, again, didn't fit a terrorist organization. How could an army like this be so well-financed and -organized and yet slip by the Alliance's sophisticated intel and tight security measures? Especially if someone as notorious as Burner was behind it all?

For the first time since we'd been captured, one of our captors finally spoke. "Which one of you is the commanding officer?" he asked. I noticed a single red strip of cloth sewn above the forehead of his robe - a symbol of rank, no doubt.

Without a second's hesitation, Bruno raised his hand. "That would be me."

"Name?" asked Red Stripe.

"Sgt. Bruno. Serial #F17099-T."

"Who's your second?"

"He is," Bruno said, pointing at me. That wasn't entirely true but no one volunteered otherwise.

"You two. This way." He nudged us deeper into the tunnel while his friends held the other Devilbats back.

Bruno and I marched ahead and Red Stripe fell into step behind us. We had to crouch to enter the tunnel and were nudged along by the barrel of Red Stripe's WarMaker pressed into our backs. I considered the odds - two of us against one of him - but I quickly dismissed any thought of taking him out. Even if we could overpower him (and I knew we could), we had no idea what lay ahead of us. And returning the way we came in would just lead us back to our own men, still under guard by terrorists with very large multi-phase weapons.

"Where are you taking us?" Bruno asked after a few moments.

"Just walk." Red Stripe was obviously under orders not to spend any quality time with us. I had a feeling that particular pleasure had been reserved for someone higher up the food chain.

Eventually the tunnel opened into a huge cavern, lined with supporting rails of supra-steel and plasti-mesh. Dozens of soldiers, minus the robes but wearing the modern war uniforms I had seen earlier, moved about the cavern busily, loading weapons, checking actions, dismantling and re-mantling rifles.

In the center of the room a stone mesa rose several feet from the floor. A wooden table sat there, and on the table was a huge paper map. Three men pored over the map, making notes occasionally and talking quietly to themselves. I was reminded of the makeshift war rooms of the ZSW and realized that was exactly what I was seeing here. A war room designed to do battle against the Galactic Alliance - a war fought not by soldiers, but a bunch of fucking cowards who would only attack innocent, unarmed civilians.

I thought again about Bruno and his theories about live versus dead soldiers and I vowed that I wouldn't leave this

93

place until I had thwarted the men on the stage before me. No matter what the cost.

Red Stripe led us over to the miniature plateau and cleared his throat. When there was no response from the men above him, he tried again. Finally, one of the men looked over. He wore a ragged New York Yankees ballcap and had a thin cigar wedged between his teeth. He wore a military uniform like the one under Red Stripe's robe, but on his shoulder were displayed three red lines, one atop the other.

"The commander of the Alliance Troops," Red Stripe announced, "And his First Officer."

The man in the Yankees cap stepped to the edge of the stage and stared down, glaring at us from above. If he hoped his level gaze would put the fear of God into Bruno and me ... well, he was wrong.

"Gentlemen," he said in a deep, well-mannered voice. "My name is Abraham Wilkinson, and I'm the commander of the base you have unsuccessfully tried to invade. I suppose one of you can tell me why the Galactic Alliance has launched an unprovoked attack on the Brotherhood of Separatists."

For more than a moment, both Bruno and I were too stunned to speak. The Brotherhood of Separatists? They were the equivalent of what used to be called a "militia" back in the 2000s. The B.O.S. was an ultra-conservative organization that didn't trust the Alliance government and decided they would rather leave Earth and start a new civilization of their own. They exercised their constitutional right to create an armory and then opted to leave Earth for greener solar systems nearly fifteen years ago. Although the government had tried to keep track of them, they had vanished completely and, in fact, were most often thought of as lost in space.

But here they were in the flesh, nestled on a planet that our intel told us was inhabited by terrorists. Terrorists who had killed over 3,000 people just a few days before.

I realized that I wasn't feeling that dull, deadly rage – at least for the moment – but it took me a moment to figure out why.

Because terrorism didn't fit the modus operandi of the Brotherhood of Separatists. They left Earth because they didn't want to become more of the "sheep" that the government led around by the nose. They left Earth because they wanted to preserve their definition of what the U.S. Constitution was all about. They left Earth because they didn't believe in an armed overthrow of the government; they believed in starting a new government of their own. Their armory and subsequent military were built only to defend them in case the Alliance government, or anyone else for that matter, decided to try and stop them.

So unless their credo had changed dramatically over the past fifteen years – and I didn't think it had or we would have been dead already - the B.O.S. weren't the terrorists we were looking for. Either our intel had made a serious error ...

... or we had been misled here intentionally.

To kill innocent people.

Or to have those innocent people kill us.

"Commander Wilkinson, I believe a terrible mistake has been made here," I said.

"That's the God's absolute truth," Wilkinson growled.

"But if you'll allow us to contact our other troops, we can still call this thing off before it gets out of control and more blood is spilled."

Wilkinson laughed. "You must think I'm pretty stupid," he said. "Think we're all a bunch of inbred cultists."

"No, sir, not at all ..."

"Let your people come," Wilkinson continued. "We'll cut them down before their feet touch the ground."

"Please, listen to me ..."

Wilkinson stood abruptly and turned away. "Dismissed!" he called out. Red Stripe was there instantly. "Get them out of here," Wilkinson ordered.

Red Stripe jabbed his gun barrel into my back. "Let's go."

But Bruno wouldn't budge. "Commander Wilkinson!" he called loudly. Wilkinson stopped and turned but Red Stripe had already taken Bruno's arm and was yanking him away.

Big mistake.

In a blur of movement, Bruno swept Red Stripe's legs out from underneath him and delivered a crushing blow to the man's chest. Gasping for breath, Red Stripe went down but he hadn't even hit the ground before Bruno snatched away the snipeblazer and pointed it directly at Wilkinson's head, his finger one RCH from pulling the trigger.

Everyone in the ill-lit cavern froze, staring from Bruno to Wilkinson, and back again. Wondering if the next moment might bring blinding violence and bloody death.

The only sound was that of water, dripping undisturbed somewhere inside the cavern.

"Commander," Bruno continued soberly, "I don't want to hurt you or anybody else here but you will be dead before anybody ..." Bruno raised his voice toward the ceiling where a sniper was fixing him in the crosshairs "... and I mean *anybody* ... can act against me. So I respectfully request that your men stand down."

Wilkinson considered for a moment, his dismay and rage at the sudden turn of events apparent. After a moment, he raised his hand into the air. "Everybody stand down," he said. Then, staring down at Bruno. "For now."

The electric tension in the room declined by a few volts but the pressure was still on. Bruno cleared his throat. "My name is Sgt. Bruno. I served in the WildeBeest Platoon during the Zombie Slave War. Some of you may have heard of me. I came here today, Commander, to destroy a nest of terrorists who are responsible for the bombing of the ZSW monument on Earth and the deaths of over 3,000 innocent people." His eyebrows narrowed in grim determination. "If I thought you and your people were responsible, Commander, I would have you all killed where you stand and - despite your macho posturing - I think you should know that there are over 140 pissed-off, fully-armed, itchin'-to-kill Alliance soldiers on their way here now and they will not be denied their unholy vengeance."

I looked up at Wilkinson to see a combination of confusion and anger fog his features. There was also a hint of fear there, but just a hint. Wilkinson was no coward. "We had nothing to do with that," he said.

"Commander, I actually believe that," Bruno answered. "I believe we were led here with a false piece of evidence, left by the real perpetrators to further blur their trail. And in the hopes of further blurring the already opaque relationship between the Galactic Alliance and the B.O.S."

Opaque? I thought. Damn, Bruno must have been doing some reading.

"And that's why I ask you, Commander, man-to-man, ZSW veteran to ZSW veteran - yes, Commander, you may not know me, but I know *you* - to let me contact my troops and put a halt to this thing before more lives are lost unnecessarily. Lost in the god damned name of terrorism."

Bruno dropped the barrel of the Snipeblazer then and gently handed it back to Red Stripe, who took it and immediately pointed it at Bruno's heart. Red Stripe probably didn't realize it but, if he pulled the trigger, he would be the second to die. I would make sure of that.

"Please, commander," Bruno continued. "If you don't let me make that call — your people will all die. Make no mistake about it."

Wilkinson stood still for a moment and every eye was on him. The water continued to *plip, plip, plip* behind him. Finally, he took a deep, careful breath.

"I'm going to take your word for this, Sgt. Bruno, because, yes, I know your name, too, sir. But, so help me God, if you're lying, your death will not be quick and painless."

"I would expect nothing less, Commander."

"Someone give him a handcom," Wilkinson ordered.

A small device was pressed into Bruno's hand. He nodded his gratitude to Wilkinson and keyed the correct code into the machine.

"Command One, this is Sgt. Bruno," he said, "Abort Operation Rat Hunt. I repeat, Abort Operation Rat Hunt. Authorization code: 7665-4977-66."

There were a few tense moments as only silence answered Bruno's request. Then, a voice buzzed through the handcom. "Bruno, this is command. Order received and accepted. Standing down and will await further orders."

Bruno tossed the handcom up to Wilkinson and nodded his gratitude. "Thank you, sir. Believe me, you've done the right thing here."

"We'll see," Wilkinson said.

CHAPTER FOURTEEN

Several hours later, after an intense period of investigations on both sides – the B.O.S. confirming that the Alliance attack was an error and not an invasion, and the Alliance confirming that the B.O.S. were not responsible for the attack on the ZSW memorial – Bruno and I found ourselves sitting across a long, whitewood table, glasses of cool, locally welled water before us, staring at Commander Wilkinson and three of his top officers.

Bruno had just completed debriefing Wilkinson on what we knew about the terrorist attack. Most of it Wilkinson had already gleaned from what he'd seen on the news and from his previous investigation.

The B.O.S. commander listened quietly, nodding his head occasionally, taking notes and following Bruno's report with the attention of a man who knew every word could be important. He wasn't just listening, he was completely absorbing everything Bruno had to say.

Bruno explained that we had no idea how the explosives had been transferred to Earth's surface without triggering the usual security alarms and Wilkinson suddenly leaned forward, his eyes tightening.

"There was no alarm at all?" he asked, stunned.

"None," Bruno confirmed. "The Powershield was in perfect working order as was the sub-shield that surrounds the city. Post-diagnostics confirm that. According to our experts, nobody could have smuggled any type of explosive into the Memorial, especially something with the destructive force of inferno technology."

"Were TP frequencies being monitored?" Wilkinson asked.

TP was short for teleportation, the science of converting solid matter into a beam of energy and then sending it from one point to another where it was re-formatted back into solid matter. TP use was strictly monitored and approved for only limited use since it didn't take long for the assholes of the world to realize they could send bombs or viruses anywhere they chose from the relative safety of their own living room.

That and the trucking industry was pissed that they were becoming obsolete.

I nodded. "Of course," I told Wilkinson. "The sub-shield is designed to locate any use of teleportation within two thousand miles of the city, from any direction. If something had been teleported, we would have been notified and disruptor sequences would have halted any unauthorized beam."

Wilkinson scratched the tip of his nose. I sensed that he had something to say but was hesitant. Finally, he said: "This may be a stupid question, but are the Powershield and sub-shields programmed to report Compressed TP as well as Standard TP?"

Bruno blinked. "What the hell is compressed TP?"

"It's a theoretical teleportation method," I said. "According to some scientists, the standard TP wave can be compressed to the wavelength of lesser standards, like television or radio, making it quicker and less costly to send and receive." I looked up at Wilkinson. "But it's just a theory. It's never actually been achieved in the lab."

"Maybe, maybe not," Wilkinson said. "We may have separated our government and our lives from Earth, Mr. Fist, but we'd be stupid to turn our backs on its technology. I remember reading recently that Compressed TP had, in fact, been achieved during a recent experiment." He paused and spoke a brief command into his computer port. "If I'm right," he continued, "Your explosives could have easily been transported to Earth this way."

A moment later, a holographic image of a magazine appeared on the table before him. I could just read its name: "Scientific Alliance." Wilkinson reached forward, and touched the pages briefly. They flipped as though they were made of paper and not of light. After a moment, Wilkinson said, "Here it is," and tapped the page in front of him. It expanded to poster size so that we could all read it clearly.

It was a recent article, published within the past eight weeks (Wilkinson hadn't been kidding when he said that the Separatists were keeping up with science). According to the article, a group of scientists at the Australian University of Higher Science had compressed a teleportation wave and beamed a candy bar from one end of the room to another. (There was no mention of what type of candy bar, but the thought of candy made me realize I was hungry). The article went on to say that previous attempts with lab rats had proven unsuccessful, with the rats suffering so many mal-aligned molecules that only one had made the short trip alive and that particular rat had perished within seven seconds of arriving at its destination. The candy bar, however, had apparently been beamed through without any sign of damage or mal-alignment.

"Does it mention any supporting studies from other labs?" I asked.

"No," Wilkinson replied. "According to the article, only A.U.H.S. is following this. They hope to bring teleportation back into common usage by making beams that are smaller and more easily secured. It'll take hundreds, if not thousands, of more successful experiments like this one before the government can re-assess whether it's safe and feasible."

"Successful being the keyword," Bruno added.

"Exactly," Wilkinson agreed. He waved his hand through the image of the article and it vanished. A moment later, a hard copy popped up through the tabletop. Wilkinson tore it free and handed it to me.

"It's one thing to beam a candy bar across a tabletop," I said. "It's something else entirely to beam a high explosive across a city and into a protected target."

"Agreed," said Bruno. "But it's definitely worth looking into."

103

"I guess that means we're going to school," I said.

"Looks that way," he agreed.

Wilkinson stood and reached across the table. His hand enveloped mine, gripped once, then released and went over to visit Bruno's. "Good luck, gentlemen. If there's anything we can do to help, please let me know."

"We will, Commander Wilkinson," Bruno said, getting to his feet. I followed his lead. "Thank you for your understanding and my deepest apologies for any trouble we've caused you here. It was never our intention to disturb the B.O.S."

"Apology accepted," Wilkinson said. "But, please, let the world know we were ready to fight. Maybe it'll give us a few more years of peace and freedom here."

CHAPTER FIFTEEN

Technically, the Australian University of Higher Science wasn't *in* Australia. It was actually deep beneath the Timor Sea, 22 miles off the coast of the continent, six miles from the shores of Melville Island. Built with funds from the governments of various nations and a huge grant from the Global Alliance, the A.U.H.S. was originally designed with deep space transportation research in mind. By building the university beneath the sea, researchers could use the surrounding waters to cool their various, heat-extreme experiments without extravagant expenses and with limited environmental invasion. As Arnold Chapel, designer of the modern flex engine, once said, "You can't get there without getting hot." Flex engine technology generates enormously high temperatures; it made sense in more ways than one to use the surrounding ocean waters as a cooling shield.

Unfortunately, the fact that the A.U.H.S. was beneath the ocean presented a problem for The Charger. Although it had been re-fitted with flex technology and upgraded for space travel, it had been too long since I last had it sea-proofed. Last year after a day of watching whales off the coast of Santa Barbara with Candy, the Charger had come out of the ocean sparking like an air raid for an hour after I hit dry land. People passing me probably thought I was celebrating Global Alliance Independence Day when, in fact, I was crossing my fingers and praying that a stray spark wouldn't set off the self-destruct mechanism.

So Bruno and I parked the Charger in the coastal city of Darwin and took a commuter bus to Melville Island. We grabbed a sandwich to eat on the run – it was made of something the locals recommended called Vegemite that tasted like ripened celery paste - and then bought a ticket for a day cab to take us to the underwater campus.

Day cabs are bluntly Spartan modes of transportation but are safe, effective, inexpensive and (most importantly in our case) fast. We stepped into the transparent, thin-shelled capsule and watched carefully as the seal re-healed itself behind us. The molded seats were hard as a rock and the air inside was stale and thick. There was a thump and a heavy click as the security devices locked into place. From this point on, we could only sit, watch and wait.

As the sun's energy baked into the transparent shell it began to flicker with the colors of the rainbow and then, suddenly – with a whoooosh! - we were off, shooting through the air at nearly 100 miles per hour. With limited inertia dampeners, the rush of speed was obvious and somewhat enjoyable. It felt a bit like riding a roller coaster.

There wasn't room in the cab to do more than sit quietly, so I did just that, whistling "Ace of Spades" and wondering how long it would take Bruno to tell me to shut the hell up.

The turquoise ocean glittered below us as the sun's rays danced off it like millions of flickering diamonds. Looking down at its cold blue beauty, it was hard to believe there were thousands of people beneath its cover, going about their daily routines as though it were just another normal day.

Of course, in their case, it was.

Four minutes later (still, disappointingly, with no musical critique from Bruno), we reached the point of entry that would take us to A.U.H.S. and the day cab went into a nose dive, hurtling downward at what seemed like breakneck speed. The impact of the cab into the water was surprisingly gentle, thanks to the combined effects of cab design and electronic shield technology. Comfortable, no. Gentle, yes.

As soon as the white water created by our entry began to fade away, the University became visible in all its glory deep beneath us. Spread out like a series of soap bubbles connected by thin, hair-like vines, the A.U.H.S. was a miracle of engineering and a wonder to behold. The main bubble was, of course, the mother dome, housing the administration and many of the classrooms. Spreading out like rays of the sun were free-flowing tubes through which day cabs - exactly like our own - zipped to and fro, carrying students and staff to their myriad destinations.

There were dozens of dorms spread out across the sea bottom (alive with vibrantly colored fauna to the credit of the university's ecology efforts). Each dorm was basically the same size - about a third of the mother dome - and each bore a letter of the Greek alphabet on its opaque glass roof. Sprinkled around these were the smallest set of domes which I assumed to be individual classrooms and smaller labs.

With the water hissing around us, the cab arched toward the mother dome and one of the many portholes built into its right side. The porthole didn't look big enough for the cab to slip through but there were other cabs ahead of us and they seemed to be going in just fine. Still, I yearned for the Charger and the huge garage I could see just behind the mother dome. It would have been far more comfortable and not nearly as nerve-wracking to put down there. On the other hand, the Charger's now famous fireworks display was something I could do without. I made a mental note to get the car into the shop as soon as possible.

Finally, our day cab slipped through its assigned porthole and fell into an inner luge. After a few seconds of gentle sliding, we slowed and came to a slippery halt inside a pressurized disembarking room. The bright light bouncing off the apparently plastic walls was somewhat of a shock after spending time in the darker ocean but it only took a moment for our eyes to adjust.

As the cab came to a smooth stop and a young greeter came to release us, Bruno grunted. "That was fun." He didn't sound like he really meant it.

"Yeah. Who needs Disneyland?"

"Not me. By the way, your 'Ace of Spades' sucks."

Our greeter was a clean-cut young man whose perfect black hair looked like it could have been detached and replaced again in one piece. A matching tuft of it hung from his lower lip. He touched an electro-key to the cab and the invisible door hissed open. His smile was so bright that my eyes had to adjust again. "Welcome to the Australian University of Higher Science," he said cheerfully and handed us each a terrycloth towel.

"What's with ...?" the towel, I started to say, then felt a few drops of water fall onto my head. Looking up, I could see the ceiling was layered with a sheen of moisture which occasionally grew a tear and dropped it on those below.

"Problem with our thermal dryer," the greeter said, shrugging. His smile never faltered.

"Problem with the thermal dryer?" Bruno asked incredulously, "Isn't this an engineering school?"

"Yes, sir," said the greeter proudly, then quietly added, "We're working on it."

As we toweled the droplets from our faces, the greeter asked us where we were headed.

"Administration," I told him. "We're here to see Vice President Kessler."

"Iris Kessler, Vice President of Academic Affairs," the greeter clarified, then lowered his voice conspiratorially. "I'll be curious to see what you think about her new 'do." Before I could ask him what he meant by that, he quickly gave us directions to Ms. Kessler's office and had already turned to welcome the next arrivals.

The walk through A.U.H.S. was lovely. The roof that appeared opaque from the outside was crystal clear from within, allowing a glorious view of the ocean around us, and the buildings and other structures were aesthetically and pleasingly designed. Using an old California style of adobe architecture as a standard, the buildings at A.U.H.S. seemed warm and homey and avoided the sterile, high-tech look one might have expected. The pastel pink coloring scheme that was the norm throughout added to the serene atmosphere.

"Nice place," Bruno agreed, keeping step. "Wonder if they're hiring."

"Probably," I replied, "But I doubt they're looking for someone who teaches Killing 101."

Bruno shrugged.

We passed a building with the words "Bi-Species Education Center" protruding from its adobe-like wall.

"Bi-Species?" Bruno said aloud.

"Yeah, it's the only place in the world where dolphins and humans are taught side-by-side," I told him. We couldn't see the interior from the path we were on, but I knew what it looked like from articles I'd read and reports I'd seen. "You should see it," I continued. "Inside, there are several rows of desks for the human students and a comfortable pool for the dolphins right beside them. The pool allows direct access from the ocean and dolphin students use it as their entrance and exit. There are two podiums in front of the student area - one the standard human lectern, the other a raised bath from which a dolphin professor can speak. The entire room is hard-wired with translators so that the humans hear human language and the dolphins hear dolphin language, simultaneously, no matter who's speaking."

It was the most advanced classroom of its kind anywhere in the universe and it was the pride of Earth since the Dolphins had been accepted into the Global Alliance sixteen years ago.

Bruno gave it a non-committal harrumph.

Finally, we arrived at a round-cornered building with smooth stone arches surrounding it. I made note of the helpful signage: "Administration." We went inside.

The attractive blonde woman at the reception desk (the faux wooden plaque there indicated her name was Sandra Jimenez) seemed young enough to belong in class rather than working in the office. She looked up when we approached and smiled one of those smiles that was just pleasant enough for visitors but wasn't the gorgeous, full-of-sun smile I was sure she reserved for friends and family. I tried to lure one of those out of her with one of my own irresistible smiles but she didn't budge. A true professional. I had to respect that.

"Good morning, gentlemen," Sandra said. "How may I help you?"

"We're here to see Vice President Kessler," I told her, turning down the wattage on that powerhouse smile of mine. Why waste it on the unappreciative? I indicated Bruno with a nod of my head. "Sgt. Bruno and Mr. H.B. Fist. We have an appointment."

"I'll let her know you're here, sir. Would you care to take a seat?" Without waiting for an answer, Sandra touched her temple, activated the switchboard, and whispered, "Your ten o'clock is here," to someone elsewhere in the building.

Bruno pulled up a sterile chair of chrome and black leather that looked as out of place here amongst the adobe as a dragon at a fireman's convention. I took what I considered to be more appropriate - a wicker chair, cushioned with fluffy white pillows. Fist, the politically correct man of action. There was a copy of "Scientific Alliance" on the table in front of us and Bruno picked it up and switched it on. He scanned through the pages quickly, then turned it off and tossed it back on the table.

"What?" I asked him, picking it up.

"Not enough celebrity gossip," he said.

A few moments later, just as I had begun reading an article called "The Possibilities and Impossibilities of Time Travel," I heard the click of heels coming our way.

"Gentlemen, I'm sorry to keep you awaiting," a voice said politely. I looked up to see a tall, regal-looking woman – just a bit shorter than my six feet, in fact – walking toward us. She wore a glimmering gray business suit that accentuated her nicely rounded curves without losing the suit's professional attitude. I switched off the magazine, stood up, and extended my hand.

But when I looked up into the welcoming face of Iris Kessler, I'm sure I gave a sudden, involuntary start. And, out of the corner of my eye, I saw Bruno do the same.

"Which one of you is Mr. Fist?" asked Kessler. She smiled politely (another smile reserved for business purposes only) and extended a thin-fingered hand with which she gripped mine.

"That'd be me," I said.

Kessler nodded gently and turned to Bruno. "So you would be Sgt. Bruno."

"Yes, I would," Bruno said flatly.

"I hope you had a pleasant trip. The day cabs aren't the most comfortable means of transportation but they get the job done." She turned and headed back the way she came. "Gentlemen, if you'll follow me."

With Kessler's eyes facing the opposite direction, I took a moment to take her in. She was prim, proper and dignified. She wore her hair in what could have been the definition of "business cut" but with a sexy edge to it as well. Her pants suit was freshly-pressed and obviously designed to exude a professional attitude with a decidedly feminine touch. When you first laid eyes on her, you knew instantly she was a college professor, administrator or upper-level business executive. She had that certain, intelligent appeal about her.

But, as your eyes moved up her smooth cheeks and past that exquisitely-coiffed haircut, you would also notice that - despite first appearances - Iris Kessler *wasn't* exactly like any other college professor, administrator or business executive.

Because the flesh of Kessler's head stopped at just above ear level and was replaced by a towering glass dome that was at least half again as long as her face. Inside that dome, floating in a transparent pool of pink liquid, tangled amidst a rat's nest of hair-thin wires and tiny micro-electronics, sat her brain, on clear display to all the world.

The greeter's words faded back into my memory. *"I'll be curious to see what you think of her new 'do."*

Bruno and I shared a quick, stunned glance and followed Kessler to her office.

"Please sit," Kessler said, dropping nimbly into a black leather chair that sat behind her massive, slickly polished, redwood desk. She indicated a pair of lesser leather chairs before it. "Get you a cup of coffee?"

"No, thank you," I replied.

"Coffee would be good," Bruno said. "No milk. No sugar." He was still a bit wide-eyed but recovering quickly.

"Black," Kessler confirmed. "A man after my own heart." She punched a button on her desk and spoke to her assistant. "Sandra, would you please bring us a couple of coffees, black."

"Right away, Ms. Kessler."

As Bruno and I settled into the assigned chairs, Kessler leaned back in hers and stared at us over steepled fingers.

Her brain sloshed back as well, coming to rest against the rear wall of the glass dome. I was glad I couldn't see it from that angle. "So what can I do for you gentlemen?"

"As you know, Ms. Kessler, the ZSW Memorial was destroyed several days ago by terrorists ..."

"Yes. How awful. I heard on the news it was someone named Wormer or something."

"Burner," I corrected. "Yes, that's correct. He's a well-known terrorist and he's taken credit for the attack. We've no reason to disbelieve him."

"I see." Kessler tipped forward, her brain now bumping against the front of the dome. I tried to keep my eyes focused on hers. "But what does this have to do with the college?" she asked. "Shouldn't you be out chasing this guy or something?"

"Actually, that's exactly what we're doing," I continued. "We're trying to understand the sequence of events that led up to the bombing - how Burner set it up, who he was working with, where he got the explosives and how he transported them planetside. Once we have the answers to those questions we hope we'll have a better idea on where to find him."

Kessler sat back again, splashing pink liquid against the crown of her dome. "Of course. I didn't mean to infer that you weren't doing all you can do. But I still don't understand what brought you here."

The office door opened and Sandra came in with a tray topped with two steaming cups. She set them on the desk and quietly left the room. Kessler gently nudged Bruno's coffee toward him and grabbed her own.

"You were saying?" Kessler prompted.

"As you know, the use of teleporters on Earth is highly regulated. In order to protect civilians, the Alliance's Powershield monitors the planet surface and surrounding atmosphere 24 hours a day, 365 days a year, searching for any indication of unauthorized teleporter usage."

"Yes, but certain areas, individuals and organizations are excluded," Kessler interjected. "For example, we have a special permit here to allow us to use teleporters within certain boundaries."

"As I said, they search for *unauthorized* usage, Ms. Kessler. It's not authorized usage that we're worried about. We think that the bomb that destroyed the ZSW may have been teleported there."

"That's not possible," Kessler said. "As you just said yourself, the Powershield scans for teleportation activity 24/7. And it's designed to immediately intercept and disrupt any unauthorized beams."

"That's true to a certain degree. The Powershield is designed to find and stop *standard* teleportation waves. They do not identify, and therefore do not stop, *compressed* TP waves." I watched her carefully for a reaction. There was none other than confusion.

"What would be the point?" Kessler asked. "Teleportation via compressed waves is only theory at the moment. We believe that it's possible but we're a long way from proving it and even farther from controlling it."

"But you're working on it."

"Yes, we're working on it. We've got an entire lab here dedicated to compressed wave TP. If we can capture and control it, it would stop the crazies from abusing it. It could re-revolutionize human transportation."

"How far are you from perfecting it?"

"*Perfecting* it?!" Kessler said, rolling her eyes in exasperation. "We haven't even been able to send *light* via compressed TP waves. We're years, maybe decades from being able to send any form of matter."

I frowned. "I'm a little confused," I told her. "I just read an article in Scientific Alliance that said you had transported a candy bar ..."

"Oh, *that* article," Ms. Kessler said. "Sloppy reporting by a sloppy reporter. He had asked for a demonstration of TP while he was here doing a story on it. We showed him a few things with standard TP waves. As you read in his article, he got it all a little confused." Sloppy reporting. Had it really come to that? Was our best lead nothing but the inaccurate words of a lazy magazine writer? I sighed deeply. Maybe we were off on another wild goose chase. "Do you know of any other way the bomb could have been transported to the Memorial?" I asked.

Kessler opened her hands. "The usual ways - via car, truck, someone carrying it in with a briefcase."

Bruno shook his head. "Nope. Security was too tight, both with manpower and with machinery. We have full

117

body scans of everyone who entered the Memorial that day. They were simultaneously beamed to Washington as each person stepped through the one and only entrance. Everyone was clean."

Kessler shrugged. "I'm sorry I couldn't have been more help, gentlemen." She stood, smoothed her suit and reached across the desk. "I wish I could do more after you've come all this way."

Bruno and I stood, taking turns gripping Kessler's hand.

"We appreciate your time," I said. Despite my best efforts, I gave her glass dome a quick glance. Bruno hadn't taken his eyes off of it the whole time.

Kessler finally caught our curiosity. She touched her fingertips to her transparent forehead. "Oh, my goodness," she exclaimed. "I'm sorry, I forgot all about this. You must've thought it was pretty strange."

Bruno and I shook our heads, denying the obvious. "No, not at all," Bruno said lamely.

"I usually explain it when I meet new people," Kessler continued. "I was so busy today, I just forgot. My apologies." She reached up and pulled back her pageboy, exposing more of her pink brain, the liquids it floated in and the micro-wires attached to its every wrinkle. "It's part of an ongoing experiment," she said. "Years ago, I was in a day cab accident. A great white shark somehow made it past our sensors and entered the path of the cabs. I had time enough to see there was going to be a collision but -

with a day cab - there's nothing you can do but close your eyes and hope for the best. There was a terrific impact and I was seriously injured. Skull fracture. Some previously irreparable brain damage. So the engineers in our bio division created the new dome for me. The wires you see monitor my life functions - the things you don't think about - breathing, sleeping, eating, etc. Otherwise, I might forget to breathe and just suffocate without realizing it. The monitors make sure that doesn't happen. The readings also help the bio boys in their studies. They claim to have made great strides in understanding the human brain because of this little contraption. We still know very little about the human brain. With this ..." She tapped the side of the dome with a pencil, "... we're hoping to learn a little more."

I nodded, impressed. Bruno needed more. "Why did they make it transparent?" he asked.

"Good question," Kessler told him. "Originally, it matched my skin color, but the size and shape of the dome made me look like a pinhead or something. So I asked them to make it transparent. That way, nobody wonders why my head is so strangely shaped."

"Good thinking," I said.

"Thank you. It saves me a lot of trouble."

"Well, again, we appreciate your time," I told her, as Bruno and I turned toward the door.

A man in a white lab coat suddenly burst in, nearly bumping into me. He hugged an old fashioned clipboard,

119

the antique kind with paper, to his chest. He was tall and lanky, skinny to the point of distraction, and his Adam's apple protruded from his throat as though a real apple had lodged there. I was sure his voice would be hugely deep even before he said, "Oh, I'm sorry. I didn't realize you were in a meeting."

"Actually, your timing couldn't be better," Kessler said to him. "This is Mr. Horatio Fist and his colleague Sgt. Bruno. Gentlemen, this is Doctor Donald Saunders, head of our Teleportation Sciences division. Don, these gentlemen were just asking me about compressed TP. They were under the impression that the bomb that destroyed the Zombie Slave War Memorial could have been delivered by compressed TP."

Saunders' lower lip moved, as though he were about to say something, and then went suddenly rigid. His eyes flicked from me, to Bruno and back to Kessler. Finally, his face relaxed a little and he said, "Well, that's impossible, of course."

"That's what I told them," Kessler fairly crowed. "We're years from even testing, right?"

Saunders' lousy poker face said he wasn't too sure of that.

"Is she right, Donald?" I asked him, watching his face closely, hunting for any twitch or tic that would tell me he knew more than he was telling. "Because, according to an article I just read in Scientific Alliance, Compressed TP is just around the corner."

Saunders' eyes opened into wide little saucers. He stared at me blankly and then blinked, hard. He turned back to Kessler. Blinked again. Obviously, he felt much more comfortable lying to her. Still, that lower lip twitched and stiffened again. After a moment, his mouth slowly peeled open. He seemed ready to say something, and I was hoping it was a full confession.

I know. I'm a dreamer.

There was a moment of uncomfortable silence so I went for the kicker. "Dr. Saunders, do you have any connection with the terrorist known as Burner?"

Saunders' eyes widened again, doe-like, and he repeated that hard blink. He took a deep breath, reached for something in his breast pocket and then suddenly backhanded the clipboard into my face. I hadn't expected that and took the edge hard. Bright white stars exploded through my vision and a bright line of pain blossomed across my forehead.

Bruno leapt, reaching for Saunders, but his coat tangled in the arm of his chair and bogged him down, giving Saunders a split second advantage. Racing out of the room, Saunders slammed the office door behind him, rattling the pictures and certificates on the walls. Bruno, having freed his troublesome coat, jerked forward and slammed against the closed door. He grunted in pain and spun back into the room.

"What ...? What ...?" Kessler was babbling. College administrators weren't normally accustomed to faculty attacking visitors, especially when those visitors were officers of the law.

I suppose it was a good thing we weren't potential benefactors, there to be wooed into a donation.

I shook my head to clear it and rubbed my knuckles across my forehead. They came back dry and I was thankful the clipboard hadn't broken the skin. I jumped to my feet, yanked the door open and leapt into the hallway. Bruno was right behind me.

"There!" he said, pointing to a white-coated figure at the end of the hall just as it disappeared into a stairwell. We raced toward the stairs.

There was no way to tell whether Saunders had gone up or down. However, once Bruno and I entered the stairwell, I held up my hand while we both froze and listened. Footsteps echoed from stairs above us. We headed that way.

Three floors up, we were just in time to see an exit door slowly hiss closed. Is that where Saunders had really gone or was he trying to lead us astray?

"You go there," I told Bruno, pointing at the door. "I'm going up." Bruno nodded and disappeared through the exit. I took the stairs two at a time.

At the next landing, I heard footsteps suddenly quicken above me. The closing door below had indeed been just a ruse. I made a note to give Saunders a kidney punch for the attempt and hoped that Bruno realized the trick and would re-group with me soon.

A few more landings and I finally arrived at the top floor. The door there was closed but it was the only place Saunders could have gone. I burst through it.

We were on the roof of the A.U.H.S. administration building, about fifteen floors above ground level and about 100 feet below the roof of the dome that enclosed the university. I held my breath, cocked my head, and listened again.

Over the sound of my pounding heart, Saunders' ragged breathing huffed from behind an air conditioning unit about thirty feet to my right. Occasionally he would take a deeper breath, trying to settle himself. It wasn't working. Not only was he breathing as loudly as an elephant in heat, I could see his shadow tilting out from behind the A/C unit.

"Saunders, there's no place else to go," I said aloud. My voice was a little husky from the run up the stairs. "Come out from behind there and let's talk."

Saunders was silent for a moment, as though debating whether or not I really knew where he was. I could picture that hard blink of his and figured he was doing a lot of it. Finally, he croaked, "No. I can't. He'll kill me." His voice was rough with exertion, too, much more so than mine.

"If he doesn't, I will. And I'm here and he's not. So you might as well come out and let me try to help you."

"You can't help me."

There was no point in lying to him. "Maybe not. Burner has people everywhere and one of them could

123

easily shank your ass while you're in prison for the murder of three thousand people. But you know what? That's what you fucking get. That's the price you pay." I took a deep breath, capping my growing anger, and tried a more diplomatic approach. "But look at it this way: If you help me nail that son of a bitch, at least you'll have an asterisk by your name. At least the universe will know that - yeah, you fucked up - but you tried to help in the end. That's the only way you'll retain even a smidgeon of dignity."

Saunders remained quiet, and I hoped that meant he was listening ... and considering. So I went on: "I'm not going to promise you a new identity or a lenient sentence or anything like that. I can't. Not for what you did. But I will promise you this: If you don't help me, you'll go down in history as a murderous criminal and the partner of a cowardly bastard of a terrorist. Your family and its name will be cursed forever. Is that how you want to be known for the rest of time, Saunders? Is it?"

He was quiet again for a moment, and then practically whispered, "No one is innocent," in a sad, beaten tone.

"You don't buy that drivel. There were nearly a thousand children under the age of 14 at the Memorial that day. One thousand kids with their entire lives ahead of them. You don't call that innocent? What did they ever do to you? What did they ever do to anyone ... to deserve *that*?"

This time, Saunders remained quiet. His breathing had evened out as well.

Behind me, the roof door snicked open.

"Got him?" Bruno asked.

I nodded. "Saunders, I'm going to assume you don't have a weapon and I'm going to come around behind you and place you under arrest. Then you and I are going back to Washington and you're going to tell us everything you know."

"I can't," Saunders' voice was barely audible. "He'll kill me. He'll kill my family."

"You can and you will," Bruno said, stepping in front of me. "Because you better be more afraid of us than of him. And we're the only ones who can protect your family."

It was silent again for a moment and then Saunders stood up from behind the A/C unit. He slowly raised his arms above his head in surrender and looked at us with sad, downcast eyes. His face was the face of a man who once thought he was being noble and brave, but now felt only shame.

"Good boy, Saunders," I said, reaching behind me to remove the magcuffs from my belt. I took a cautious step forward. "Let's go get a cup of coffee and we can talk about this ..."

"You'll never stop him," Saunders said a little more loudly, his voice a scary, zombie-like monotone. "The sky is going to burn."

"What the hell does that mean?" Bruno asked.

In reply, Saunders mouth became a determined straight line. He took another deep breath ...

125

... and there was a sudden, blinding white flash.

Something hit me like a jackhammer to the chest and slammed me back into the wall. I felt the air pushed out of my lungs like a giant hand had crushed my torso. Stars flashed again as my head cracked against cement. I heard Bruno grunt as he slammed down beside me. A split second later, I realized I was coated in thick, red blood, scattered entrails and shattered bits of bone and flesh.

There was a second of complete and utter silence.

I looked over at Bruno. My entire body screamed in pain. It was as if I'd just been beaten with padlocks wrapped in a gym towel. "You okay?" I rasped.

There was nothing for five full seconds. "I've been better," Bruno croaked at last, wiggling his right arm and wincing at the broken bone that had stabbed through the skin and now protruded like an ivory spear. "Shit."

I winced. "Shit is right."

I forced myself up on my elbows and looked over to where Saunders had been just a split second before. The ground was painted with a brilliant red flower. It looked as though someone had filled a giant balloon with chum and dropped it on the roof.

Rather than face the fury of Burner, Saunders had blown himself to pieces. Probably with a bomb supplied by Burner himself.

I cursed, angry at the outcome. The entire scenario replayed in my mind at high speed as I examined every direction I could have taken. Would a different approach have changed the end result? Was there something I could have done or said that would have kept Saunders alive?

Probably not.

I stared up at the dome curved above me. As near as I could tell, there were no cracks or leaks. That was good news. Things could have been a lot worse.

In the distance, sirens began to wail. They weren't the sirens you'd expect to hear from a brawny patrol car, but rather the tinny, flat sirens you might expect from a golf cart. Campus police, I figured.

I blinked my eyes, trying to clear them of the coating of quickly coagulating goo that was formerly part of Saunders. I took a deep breath and stiffened as another jab of pain surged through me.

"I'll go get help," I said. But my arms wouldn't work and all I could do was lay there and writhe helplessly.

"Don't bother on account of me," said Bruno, and then he passed out clean.

I took another deep breath and blinding pain stabbed into my left side.

The roof door suddenly burst open and a trio of white-suited medics rushed in. Behind them were a pair of black-suited campus cops. There was a comedic moment as they hit the blood slick, realized what it was, and then nearly fell in it as they back-pedaled to get away. It was something out of an R-rated Looney Tunes cartoon and, if my face didn't feel as though I'd laid out in the sun for a week with no sunscreen on, I might have smiled.

BURNER

They were talking to me but I was beyond listening. My ears felt as though they were stuffed with cotton. Unconsciousness won out over consciousness and everything around me faded to black.

My last thought before giving into oblivion was to remind myself about the burning sky.

CHAPTER SIXTEEN

When next I opened my eyes, I found myself on a hard metal gurney in a stark, white room, blindingly lit and packed with shiny chrome instruments. The chemical scent of antiseptic filled the air.

A hospital.

A glass-encased brain sloshed in its dome at my side. I turned to find Iris Kessler sitting there beside me. Her eyes were red, swollen and wet with tears but, from the sight of her tightly clenched jaw, I didn't think she'd been crying. Those were tears of rage, disappointment and betrayal glistening in her eyes.

She caught my glance and reached out to gently touch my shoulder. It hurt a little but, being the tough guy I am, I didn't even wince. "I'm so sorry, Mr. Fist," she said. "If we had any idea that Saunders was working with terrorists ..." She broke off and her jaw tightened again.

"I know," I told her.

"We'll cooperate fully and completely, of course," she said. "This is a huge black mark against us." She dropped her face into her hands and her shoulders shook with sudden, racking sobs. "My god," she whispered. "All those people."

I put my hand on hers. More pain. My skin felt as though it had been browned in a toaster. I glanced around the room. No clock. "How long have I been out?"

"A couple of hours," she said.

"Bruno?"

"He'll be all right. He was hurt a little worse than you were - a compound fracture to the arm, some minor burns and lacerations — but he's being well taken care of."

"What's been happening?" I asked her.

"We searched Dr. Saunders' lab," Kessler continued, sitting up, rubbing tears away from her cheeks. "We found some research that he'd been keeping to himself. It was hidden on a data chad."

"Compressed TP?"

She nodded grimly. "I'm afraid so. He'd apparently been successful at it for some time, after all."

"So, that reporter was right."

"More so than I could have imagined," Kessler continued. "We found records of the successful teleportation of everything from toys to live rabbits ..."

"Bombs?" I asked.

"No." She shook her head sadly and closed her eyes. "But he had the technology."

"People?"

"It's possible."

Not what I wanted to hear. I nodded my gratitude. And then something floated back into my memory.

"The sky ..." I murmured, and Kessler looked at me curiously. "Ms. Kessler, does the phrase 'The sky is going to burn' mean anything to you?"

Kessler shook her head. "Except for the Chicken Little story," she said. "No."

"That was 'fall.' This is 'burn.' The sky is going to burn."

"In that case, no."

"Did you find anything referring to that phrase on Saunders' computer?"

"Well, no. But we weren't really looking for something like that." Her brow furrowed. "Why do you ask?"

"It was one of the last things Saunders said before he killed himself." I pushed myself up on one elbow. It hurt like a bitch, but not as much as it had two hours ago. "Ms. Kessler, I need two things right now. First, I need a companel. Then, I need to see Saunders' office and lab."

"The doctor said you weren't to move for at least twenty-four hours."

"I don't have the luxury of time, Ms. Kessler." I sat up, fought through the wave of pain that pricked me from every part of my body, and swung my legs over the side. I took my time standing, making sure that I actually could. It only took a moment for me to feel fairly secure.

"Please," I said, "I need to get moving now."

Kessler led me to a private companel booth and I called Washington. I took only long enough to fill Boris in on what had transpired here (he knew most of it already from media reports) and to tell him to immediately inform the President to start work on re-configuring the Earth's Powershields to block and report any compressed teleportation activity. If it worked once for Burner, he'd try it again. We had to close down that avenue of destruction as quickly as possible. Despite Boris' promises, I knew it could still be weeks before it was completed.

I also asked him to research the phrase "The sky is burning" and, when he mentioned Chicken Little, I asked him to repeat the phrase to make sure he had it right.

Then, Iris Kessler escorted me to Dr. Saunders' office.

♣

It has been said that a cluttered office is the sign of a brilliant mind. If that were true, then Dr. Saunders must have been a freaking genius.

His office was little more than a glorified cubicle. Four walls, a single door, a bookshelf. One of the walls was glass from floor to ceiling offering a dim, underwater view of another lab building no more than a dozen feet away. Occasionally, a silvery fish twinkled by. The people in the office across from us stared through the clear blue waters and wondered what we were up to.

Empty cardboard boxes of various sizes, that – judging from their outside labeling – had once held lab electronics or science books, were piled to the ceiling. A small refrigerator hummed in one corner.

A bulky wooden desk rested in the middle of the room, and on top of it were a small companel and a personal NeuWorld access port. A glossy black coffee cup full of pencils sat to the right of the desk. Its counterpart, a coffee-stained mountain of papers apparently waiting to be filed, was stacked on the left. A gray filing cabinet stood stoically in the far corner of the room.

The only personal items there were a photo of Mind-flick star Amber Chapel, a small card reminding Saunders of a dental appointment two weeks away (that was one appointment he wasn't going to make), a beverage cup with the logo of a popular rock'n'roll band silkscreened on it and several small toys. The toys were action figures, for the most part, and included a shiny brown dog, a wrinkled black monkey, a luxury skycar (the likes of which an interstellar spy would drive), and a scale model of an orbital cargo vessel, its model number, ORB-12-7, painted clearly on its wings. These were the kind of cheap plastic toys that came with a kid's meal at fast food restaurants. The exception was the cargo vessel, which was an expensive collector's toy, designed to sit on grown men's mantles as a tribute to their lost but not forgotten childhoods.

I took a seat at the desk and had to re-adjust the inexpensive but comfortable chair. Dr. Saunders had been a good three inches shorter than me and my knees bumped beneath the desktop.

"Can I see the chad?" I asked.

"Of course." Kessler snatched the cup of pencils from the desktop and, holding the pencils with her right hand, used her left hand to pry a small object from the bottom of the cup. She passed the object to me.

It was a data chad.

"We put it back where we found it," she said. "We thought that might be important."

I nodded and pressed the chad into the NeuWorld data slot. Three words immediately flashed on the screen: "Immersive or 2-D?"

I looked up at Kessler.

"2-D is fine," she said. "It's mostly formulas, anyway."

I tapped the key for 2-D and a series of flowing numbers and equations suddenly filled the air before me. I paged through them quickly, seeing a "4" here and an "x" there, but the math was well beyond my shaky understanding of basic algebra.

"These are compressed TP equations?" I asked Kessler.

"They are," she said. "We had them extracted and our other scientists are going over them now."

"Will this information be helpful?"

Kessler looked at me as though I were daft. "Oh, yes," she said. "If Saunders' theories prove to be accurate and sound, compressed TP will change the way goods are delivered throughout the universe ... with no more fear of abuse or terrorism."

"Once we get the Powershield updated."

"Yes. Once that's completed."

I nodded and turned my attention back to the formulas. Numbers, letters and symbols continued to fly past at a numbing rate. Nothing made a lick of sense to me.

Finally, it just stopped.

"That's it?" I asked.

"That's it," Kessler confirmed. She reached up with her right hand and scratched the glass dome of her skull. If I hadn't been so pressed for time, I would have asked her how it could have itched.

"I suppose you've been through his lab, too," I asked.

"Of course," Kessler said. "We didn't find anything out of the norm there."

"That makes sense," I said. "He wouldn't have left anything incriminating there. It's a shared lab, right?"

Kessler nodded. "He couldn't have kept anything hidden there for long."

I picked up the pencil cup and studied its base. Saunders had designed a clever compartment in the bottom of the cup that allowed the secret chad to be snapped into place there, hidden from prying eyes, yet readily available should he need it.

"If he hid the chad like this," I said, indicating the pencil cup, "Then he very well might have hidden other things elsewhere."

"We've been through this room very thoroughly," Kessler said. "Both physically and with electronics."

"I don't doubt that," I told her, "But a fresh perspective can't hurt."

I began funneling through the stuff on the desktop: the papers stacked for filing (nothing there), the logoed beverage cup (I didn't know who Dead Meat were, but they looked like unsavory characters ... my kind of band) and the desk drawers (a small bottle of economy Reyes Cartel tequila and lots more paperwork, none of it useful). I stood and started going through the empty cardboard boxes against the wall.

"We've been through all of those," Kessler reminded me. "I know you want to be thorough, but I don't want you to waste your time."

I nodded and pulled at the next box. Like a bad game of Jenga, I pulled the wrong one and the stack fell sloppily around me. I spat out a brief, unintelligible curse.

One of the boxes glanced off my shoulder and fell against the desk. The plastic dog there fell on its side, the monkey fell on its back, the luxury car slid on its four wheels about an inch, and the cargo vessel wobbled and then finally came down on its left wing...

...And its tiny cargo bay door popped open and about a hundred ball bearings rolled out onto the desk, raced for the edge and fell to the carpet below.

I steadied the boxes and returned to the desk. My boots crunched on the layer of BBs now littering the carpet.

My eyebrows came together.

"Why would there be BBs in here?" I wondered aloud.

Kessler shrugged. "To make it heavier, maybe balance it out."

I picked up the cargo vessel toy, hefted it. It was made of some kind of die cast metal. It was heavy and solid. The

136

ball bearings served no purpose that I could divine.

The sky is burning. The phrase floated through my mind. And then I froze, and my blood chilled.

"Ms. Kessler," I said softly, "I'm going to need to call Washington again. And I need someone to bring me my car from the mainland. *Now.*"

CHAPTER SEVENTEEN

Campus security had disabled Dr. Saunders' companel so we raced back to the administration building. Kessler stopped only long enough to send her assistant for my car in Darwin and we continued immediately to her office. Without asking, I plopped down behind her desk and quickly dialed Boris's direct line. Kessler watched me with concerned eyes.

Boris seemed surprised to see me. "H.B.," he said as his image flicked onto the screen, "How are you feel...

"Never mind that," I told him, "I think another attack is imminent. I need to know how many cargo ships are in orbit around the planet at this very moment."

"Cargo ships?" Boris asked, confused. "But there must be hundreds of them."

"Pull up anything that's the size of an ORB-12-7 and bigger," I spat. "We need to know now, Boris."

Boris barked orders to the wall of intel geeks behind him and a few painfully slow moments crept by as the data was fed into their handports. Finally, the information he had requested popped up on Boris' screen. "There are 38 total," Boris told me. "Sixteen are ORB-12-7's, six are ORB-14-7's and twelve are the new ORB-15-8's."

"Dammit! That's too many!" I crashed my fist down

on the desk. Kessler flinched. I took a quick, deep breath and steadied myself. "Boris, can you tell me what's in their holds?"

"We can try." He turned and set the intel geeks back to work. I could see their fingers dancing on their handports and see their lips twitching as they spoke into head mikes. A few even more painfully empty moments stretched by, then Boris's screen lit up again and he started reading the list aloud. "Food, clothing, companel components, furniture, automobiles ..."

"Wait," I said. "What kind of automobiles?"

Boris did some quick finger tapping. "Atoyat trucks," he said. "And PodPorters."

PodPorters. Spherical little transports designed specifically for quick trips to and from the Moon Mall. About the size of an old style Volkswagen Beetle but with anit-grav units replacing the archaic wheels. Specifically designed to withstand the high temperatures of re-entry.

And shaped exactly like a ball bearing.

"That it!" I exclaimed. "That's it, Boris! How many PodPorters are onboard?"

He glanced at the screen again. "Thirteen hundred," he said.

"They're going to release those PodPorters into the atmosphere, Boris. They're going to drop them like thirteen hundred little meteors."

Boris sat back and stared at me, stunned. "My God."

"That's what he meant by 'The Sky is Burning,' Boris.

Without the proper shielding and force dampening equipment, those things will light up like Roman candles."

"But they won't burn up before they hit the ground," Boris said numbly.

"That right. They're designed not to," I said. "It'll be a rain of fire from the sky."

"If they hit a populated area ..." Boris started. His voice trailed off as he imagined the devastation.

"You can bet that's what they want to hit." I said. "Can you calculate potential trajectories?"

Boris turned to a thin, pale man who was apparently the head intel geek and repeated the question.

"Why, yes," the geek replied, "I can create a formula using the speed and course of the cargo ship to determine where the PodPorters are most likely to be released." His fingers flailed on the keyboard again.

I turned my attention to Kessler, who sat in front of me in open-mouthed horror. "My car?" I asked.

After a stunned second, she said: "It should be here any minute."

"Boris, I need you to transmit the location coordinates of that cargo ship to the Charger's computer."

"On their way." He paused a moment, looked up at me soberly. "You know we may have to shoot it down."

"We can't," I told him. "If we do that, we run the risk of doing their job for them."

There are moments in life, especially under extreme circumstances, when something so unexpected yet so welcome happens that one is apt to believe in divine intervention. One of those moments occurred as I stood and stepped to the doorway, on my way to the debarking garage to pick up the Charger.

Because that's when Sgt. Bruno limped through the doorway, his arm in a cast, his face the color of a freshly-boiled lobster.

"We going somewhere?" he asked.

I said, "Yeah," and gave him a grim grin.

CHAPTER EIGHTEEN

The Charger burst out of the Australian sea spitting sparks like a welding torch gone wild.

"Probably should get this thing serviced," Bruno said matter-of-factly.

I nodded. "Thank God you're here," I told him. "Otherwise, I may never have noticed."

Iris Kessler had been true to her word and the Charger had been waiting for us. There was no time to waste so we had just jumped in, started her up and headed for the sky.

As we soared over the unsuspecting Indian Ocean, I filled Bruno in on what I'd discovered in Dr. Saunders' office. He mumbled a dirty laundry list of obscene words and immediately tapped into the Charger's onboard computer to see what he could find. Boris had transmitted all the necessary coordinates to the Charger's navcom, and we were just minutes away from the cargo vessel at atmospheric speeds. We had discussed the possibility of attempting to contact the freighter and decided against it. If we tipped our hat too soon they could dump their cargo early, trying to inflict as much damage as possible before we shut them down.

If we could shut them down.

Bruno was examining the cargo ship's schematics as we rocketed toward their position. "Can you give me a flyby?"

he asked.

"I think so. But it'll risk our being seen."

"According to this, it'll take them at least ten or fifteen minutes to fully open the cargo doors and start dumping cars. Assuming they haven't started already."

"So, if they haven't started, we catch a little break."

"From what I've read here, that's the only one," Bruno said. "Unless I see something different on the flyby."

His tone made me look over.

"Yeah," he said, shaking his head. "Unless we find some other way, I don't know how we're going to stop them, short of blowing them out of the sky."

"And we can't do that," I reminded him. "Because the results will be the same."

"Yep."

"Shit."

"Yep."

I glanced down at the clock built into the Charger's dash. "We should be within visual range in a minute or so."

Bruno scanned the sky. "I don't see anything yet."

The final sparks had stopped spewing from the Charger's hood, probably because all of the water had been blown off as the car zipped through the air. The lack of sparks didn't give me any comfort, however. Unless we could figure out a way to stop Burner from dumping those vehicles into the atmosphere, thousands of people were going to die.

"There it is!" Bruno suddenly shouted. He pointed

143

through the windshield at a speck in the sky that was gradually growing as we watched. It was a long, cigar-like shape and it was moving so slowly it almost seemed to be hovering. At the moment, it looked like only a huge shadow but, as we raced closer, details of the ship's design started becoming clear. Eventually, I could see interlocking plates, hundreds of small windows, and the giant hinge on the bottom of the vehicle that would open when the ship took to port. It looked like the mouth of a giant robot dog. This is where the cars would normally be unloaded to be shipped off to dealers. "Normally" meaning not at high altitude, and not dropping from space like fiery rocks of death.

"Fly by the cargo door," Bruno said.

"Way ahead of you," I told him.

The ship continued to grow in our eyes as we got closer and closer. The nearer we got, the more I realized how huge the frigging thing actually was. It hovered over us as though it were a gray whale and we were a lamprey eel. I stomped on the accelerator and the Charger raced forward. Bruno's eyes danced across the surface of the massive cargo ship, taking in every inch and trying to deduce a way to stop the terrorists from dropping their deadly payload. He only took his eyes off the vessel long enough to page through the schematics Boris had sent us.

"Well?" I said, as we sped past the freighter and I started a wide U-turn and headed back toward it. "You got something?"

Bruno frowned. "I got something," he said. "But you ain't gonna like it."

"Tell me."

But before he could, a thousand red lights started flashing all across the freighter's body, most of them flickering around the cargo door. What looked like a giant screw head near the back of the door started rotating slowly counter-clockwise.

"Uh-oh," Bruno began. "I think ..."

"...they've started," I finished for him. "So we've got about ten minutes. Tell me your idea, now!"

"You ain't gonna like it," Bruno repeated.

"I got that part!" I snapped. "Now tell me what we have to do!"

Bruno opened the schematic blueprint of the freighter and spread it wide using his left and right thumbs. He dragged it across the windshield of the Charger until the electronic image flickered there in front of me. He pointed at the place where the robot dog's mouth would be.

"This is the cargo hold door," Bruno said. "It's the only door big enough to release even one of those little cars."

"Okay," I said. "So we've got to keep that door from opening."

"Right," Bruno agreed. "And we don't have any override codes and we can't shoot the fucker down."

"Right."

"So the only way to stop them from dumping their

145

payload is to make sure that door stays closed."

"I think I just said that."

"And I can only think of one way to do it..."

I looked forward at the cargo door. It was slowly creeping open. I could see the shiny little forms of hundreds of brand new PodPorters through the widening crack.

"We're running out of time, Sergeant," I said.

Bruno tapped an image of the screw head on the blueprint. "This wheel is both the main gear and the safety lock for the door," Bruno continued. "Hit it hard enough and it will clamp down so that the door won't open at all. For anything."

I punched the button on the dashboard that brought up the weapons console. It popped up and out and lit up like a deadly Christmas tree.

But Bruno quickly pushed it back in again.

"You can't use the onboard missiles," he said. "They're Mach 5 warheads. They'll blow that door clean off and maybe send the ship crashing down."

"So, we'll re-key them," I said. "Set the warhead for Mach two or three."

"No time," Bruno said, and I knew he was right. It would take us twenty minutes to rekey a missile's computerized explosive payload with the precision we needed. From the looks of the cargo ship's opening maw, we had maybe four or five minutes tops.

"So what the fuck do we do!?" I cried.

146

Bruno looked at me solemnly. "This is the part you're not going to like."

"I don't like any of it!"

"You've got to ram it."

I knew I must have misheard him. "I'm sorry?"

"You've got to ram it," Bruno repeated. "You've got to ram your car into that gear. The impact will set off the safety alarm and the door will stop opening."

"Ram it?" I said. "How hard?"

"I've done some quick calculations," Bruno replied. "You've got to hit it traveling approximately 88 miles per hour."

"Eighty-eight miles an hour!" I cried. "That's land speed! Even with the space travel retro-fit, it'll probably kill us."

"Might," Bruno admitted.

"There's got to be another way."

"Maybe," Bruno said. "But can we come up with it in less than three minutes?" He pointed at the cargo door. It seemed to be opening even more quickly now. The sea of PodPorters stood ready to become deadly bombs.

"You're sure?" I asked Bruno.

"I'm sure," he said.

"Well, then," I told him. "It's been nice serving with you, ya crusty ol' son of a bitch."

And I turned the wheel toward the slowly rotating door hinge.

CHAPTER NINETEEN

The next few seconds passed by in a sludgy blur. It seemed as though time were accelerating and decelerating simultaneously. I had my right foot pedal to the metal on the Charger's accelerator while my left foot toggled the brake. Trying to get to exactly 88 miles per hour, especially when the Charger was designed to go much, much faster, was going to be a challenge.

The freighter loomed larger and larger in front of us. Faster and faster. Closer and closer.

Bruno leaned over and punched in a quick code. I saw the "Virtual Airbags" light go full green. He had transferred most of the car's power to the safety systems. Good thinking.

I glanced at the speedometer. 102 mph. Too fast, yet it seemed we were crawling. I shook that illusion off and pressed the brake. If we slowed at all, I couldn't tell. The freighter now filled the entire windshield.

"Don't fuck it up!" Bruno said.

"Now you tell me!"

My eyes were locked on the giant screw head that grew larger and larger in my vision. There was no point in looking anywhere else. That was my target. That was my goal. I was still aware, however, of the ship's maw continuing to open, ready to dump out its belly full of soon to be fiery death.

We were past the point of no return. Even if I slammed on the brakes now, we were going into the freighter. We were so close now, I could no longer see anything but the wall of the freighter in front of us. The sky seemed to have disappeared behind it.

"Hold on!" I cried out.

And then everything went black.

♣

I awoke to the acrid smell of smoke stinging my sinuses and a wave of pain that washed over me and focused on a half dozen spots in my body. My eyes were filled with a sticky liquid which was either blood or window-washer fluid. I was betting it wasn't window-washer fluid. I couldn't even begin to guess how long I'd been out.

I cranked my head over and looked at Bruno's side of the car. Broken glass fell out of my hair and onto the seat. More pains shot through still other parts of my body. I felt hot wetness in other places and knew I was bleeding there, too. I hoped it wasn't too severe.

Bruno's side of the car was empty. The door hung open and I found myself staring out into an empty space that led ten thousand feet down to cold hard Earth.

Something creaked and I realized that the Charger was wedged into the corner of the main gear and the opening door. Everything looked as though it was ready to fall apart but it was holding ... for now. More importantly, the massive door had stopped opening. It was locked down tight.

Bruno had been right. We had stopped the PodPorters from falling.

Suddenly, a hand reached through the shattered windshield and grabbed my shoulder. I turned quickly, ready to deliver a solid fist to somebody's unsuspecting chin, but my shoulder didn't cooperate and my arm fell limply to its side.

"Come on, boy," Bruno said, taking a handful of my shirt and pulling me through the windshield. "We ain't done here yet."

I scrabbled across the hood of the Charger and sat there a moment, getting my senses about me. Bruno gave me a few seconds and then said, "Come on. We gotta go."

"Go where?"

"This is fuckin' weird," Bruno said. "But we're the only living things on this ship."

"What?"

"I checked the ship computer. No life signs, anywhere on board. And everything's set to auto-pilot. We're gonna have to disable the auto-pilot to land her. No biggie. I can handle that. But that ain't all."

"What else?"

"Follow me and I'll show you."

Bruno led me past row after row of PodPorters until we came to a Companel wall. Across the 'panel's keyboard, somebody had written in white spray paint: "Play Me" and drawn a white arrow to the ENTER key. A test pattern on the viewscreen told me a video was cued to play there.

I looked at Bruno. "Could be a trap. Start a self-destruct sequence."

"Could be."

"Did you try it?" I asked.

He shrugged. "Nope. I'm retired. You're still on the government dole. You try it."

"I hope it's an Amber Chapel 'flick" I said.

"You and me both. But I ain't holding my breath."

Reluctantly, I reached out and tapped the ENTER key.

The test pattern dissolved into static for a moment and then an image of a man faded onto the screen. The shock of orange hair told me instantly who it was. And, just as instantly, I knew we were in trouble.

"If you found this," said the terrorist known as Burner from the viewscreen, "Then you probably found a way to put a stop to my special gift to Earth." He stopped and clapped his hands in the same annoying way they do it in the MindFlicks. Once, then again and again and again, faster and faster until, suddenly, he stopped. "No matter. As much as I would have liked to have seen the fireworks, all of this actually works better as a distraction."

Bruno and I exchanged uneasy glances.

Burner continued: "You see, while you were expending all your time and energy trying to stop the sky from burning, I've been kidnapping various members of the

151

White House staff. By the time you get this little missive, a dozen of the most important people on the planet will have suddenly disappeared. No, no. Don't worry. They're all safe for the moment. And I'm willing to return them if the price is right. Ironic, isn't it? The only way you're going to get your people back is to fund my war against you. Of course, if we can't negotiate a fair price, well, then, I'm afraid those twelve fabulous public servants will all suffer the same fate as this gentleman. Perhaps you've seen him on your Companel at home? His name is Colin Marlowe and he is the White House Press Secretary."

The image suddenly switched to an image of Colin Marlowe. I recognized him instantly. He and I had had many engaging conversations over the years at White House events that Candy had been invited to. I was used to seeing him in a way-too-expensive suit, his face perfectly made up and with his white hair expertly coiffed. Now, however, he was standing behind a wall of glass in an unidentifiable chamber, his arms tied behind him, his hair and eyes wild. He looked to be wearing some kind of anonymous jumpsuit. A cold spot grew in my belly as I realized this wasn't going to be good.

"What is that?" I asked out loud.

"A retort chamber," Bruno said hollowly. "For cremations."

I looked at him in disbelief. He only shook his head sadly.

A moment later, the walls of the chamber began to

glow. They went from a cool sea blue to a warm, sunny yellow to a malevolent orange to a violent red. Marlowe began to panic. Dark patches appeared under his arms and around his neckline as the temperature in the room increased at an alarming rate. He seemed to have trouble breathing as air inside got hotter and hotter. The red walls gave way to white hot, and Marlowe began screaming as small fires began to burst out on his jumpsuit. Then, suddenly, the room exploded into a ball of flame and Marlowe was swallowed where he stood. Another moment passed, the oxygen was sucked out of the room and the flames died out almost instantly.

All that remained was a man-sized carpet of blackened ash.

I heard Bruno give a low growl of pure rage behind me.

There was a burst of static and the image of Burner returned. "Let's get to the bargaining table and come up with a fair number," he said. "Otherwise, these fine twelve servants of the Global Alliance ... oh, I'm sorry, make that *eleven* servants ... will suffer the same fate." He gave the screen a friendly smile and glanced at a wrist chronometer. "I'll be in touch, say, at about 1:00 PM, Eastern Time. Talk to you then."

And the screen went black.

The pain in my arm suddenly meant nothing as I scrambled for the handcom on my belt. I yanked it from its holster and quickly dialed my home number.

"What?" Bruno said. And then stopped, coming to the

same conclusion himself.

There was no answer at home.

I closed the call and dialed Candy's office line. Her assistant, Kristyn Rickman, answered it on the first ring.

"Kristyn, it's H.B.," I said quickly. "Where's Candy?"

"She hasn't been in all day," Kristyn told me worriedly. "We were hoping you knew."

I slammed the phone closed and barely resisted the temptation to throw it across the ship.

"He's got her," I told Bruno helplessly. "Goddammit, Bruno, Burner's got my wife."

CHAPTER TWENTY

It was all confirmed in the next hour or so. Twelve members of the White House staff seemed to have simply vanished. Most of them had left for work that morning but never made it to the office. Others had gone out to lunch and simply not returned. By the time anyone realized something nefarious was afoot, it was too late. They had already been taken.

And now one of them was dead and the others were being lined up to follow suit.

And one of them was my wife.

Burner had my wife.

And he had just made the biggest mistake of his life.

♣

The President had sent a team of marines to bring the booby-trapped freighter safely to the ground as well as a transport to take Bruno and I back to the Pentagon. The Charger wasn't going anywhere – it was toast. As much as I loved that car, that simply didn't matter right now. Only Candy did.

Just before we strapped in for the short ride to the Pentagon, my handcom rang. It was Iris Kessler.

"Mr. Fist, would it be possible for you to return to

A.U.H.S.? I think I've discovered something that will help you in your investigation."

"I'm on the way to Washington to meet with the President," I told her. "Unless you've got Burner's home address, I can't make it."

"How about the next best thing?"

My eyebrows shot up. "What have you got?"

"I don't think we should discuss this over an open line," Kessler said.

She was right. For all we knew the communication lines at the University were being monitored by Burner himself. "We'll be there in half an hour or less."

"That will be fine."

♣

We met briefly with Kessler and I left Bruno there to do some follow-up with her while I returned to the War Room in Washington, DC. I walked in the door and found myself staring at a roomful of grim, agitated faces. Everyone seemed to be talking at once and nobody seemed to be listening.

Boris rolled over, his pulleys and scaffolding squeaking and twisting. He extended a balloon-fingered hand.

"H.B., I'm so sorry."

"I appreciate that, Boris."

"How are you holding up?"

"Not very goddamned well."

"I can't even imagine. If there's anything I can do ...?"

"Let's just find this son of a bitch," I said.

"We will." He gave my hand a final squeeze, turned and whirred away.

It was 12:45 PM. Fifteen minutes until Burner's call.

I knew I had to stay cool. I knew I had to stay calm. A reviled anti-Alliance terrorist was holding my wife hostage and I knew how things had to be played. The Alliance didn't negotiate with terrorists. They couldn't. Negotiate with one and they all come running, bombs strapped to their chests, hands out for a donation. There would be no negotiation. The fact that he had my own wife – along with ten other high-ranking members of the White House staff – didn't change that one damn bit.

Which didn't make being cool and calm any easier.

The waiting was excruciating. What would Burner's next move be? What would he demand now? I didn't have a clue. But I knew this much: The son of a bitch was going to pay. And, if he touched one auburn hair on Candy's head, he was going to die. And die badly.

I took a seat at a table near the President and tried to calm my breathing. It was no use. The only way I would get back to normal would be to have Candy safely by my side and Burner's flapjack cel tight in my fist.

I glanced toward the main entrance, hoping that Bruno had returned from Australia, but there was no sign of him. He couldn't be too far behind me. He was going to spend an hour tops with Kessler and then join me, hopefully in

157

time for Burner's next presentation. I would have felt better with his battle-hardened assurance beside me. But what Kessler had told us was important enough that Bruno stay to see it through. So here I was alone, anxiously awaiting word of my beloved wife's fate.

The President cracked his gavel on the desktop and the room slowly began to quiet. A few more hammered staccatos and he got the silence he wanted. "We've got about ten minutes until we're supposed to hear from Burner again," he said. "Does anybody have anything new to say?" A roar of voices assaulted him. He cocked his head angrily and stopped, taking a moment to gather his patience. He held up a silencing hand. "I mean anything *constructive?*" he added.

General Dalton raised his hand and then stood up to his full, 5' 6" height. He was still the most solid looking man I'd ever seen. "Mr. President, we're going to try again to triangulate Burner's position based on his transmission." A mild uproar buzzed through the crowd and it was Dalton's turn to hold up a hand for silence. "We realize he's been hiding his signal, but we've got a few tricks of our own. I am of the mind that *any* information we can glean from this attempt will be worth the effort."

"And what if you can actually pinpoint his location?" the President asked.

"Then, sir, we will be scrambled and ready to attack that position in a matter of moments."

I suddenly found myself on my feet. "What about the

hostages?" I demanded. In my ears, my voice sounded weak and strained. I knew the answer to the question even before Dalton replied.

"I truly understand your concern, Mr. Fist, and we'll do everything we can to protect them. But I'm sure you understand and appreciate that any chance we get to hit Burner must be taken."

I took a deep, shaking breath. "I understand it," I said. "But I'm not exactly confident about its success considering how little we've achieved so far. I think we should listen to what the bastard has to say before we make any rash decisions."

"I'm sorry that your wife was taken, Mr. Fist," said the President from his podium. "We all share your concern for her safety and the safety of the others. And we will do what we can to keep them out of harm's way. But the Global Alliance does not negotiate with terrorists. The precedent that would set would bring them spilling out of the woodwork."

"That's easy for you to say," I told him. "Your wife isn't being held at gunpoint by that fucking psycho."

"That's enough, Mr. Fist!" snarled another voice. It was Colin Hancock, of course, and he was trying to play the tough guy. It was kind of cute. "You will address the President in the tone and manner in which he deserves. Otherwise, you will be asked to leave these proceedings."

I didn't want to be thrown out before Burner made his call or I would have probably spat in Hancock's face.

Instead, I forced myself to relax, and eased slowly back into my chair. "My apologies, Mr. President," I said. "My nerves are understandably jangled."

I took a sip of water from the glass on my table and felt someone slide into the chair beside me. It was Bruno. He shot me a supporting smile and then reached up and put his hand on my shoulder, an old friend comforting another in need.

Of course, it had nothing to do with that. It was his way of telling me that things had gone well in Australia and we had to get out of here as soon as possible. It was great theater. Where were the critics when you needed them?

I looked up at the clock just above the President's head. The digital counters clicked over to 12:59 PM. Any minute now, assuming he made good on his promise, Burner would begin his transmission.

As if on cue, one of the President's many underlings entered the room. "Sir?"

The President nodded grimly. "Put it on," he said.

The giant companel screen behind the President crackled with static for a moment and suddenly, there was Burner. Not a single strand of orange hair was out of place and the smile on his face resembled a disturbed, yellow-fleshed Jack O'Lantern. His smug grin made me realize that the sick bastard was having the time of his life.

Enjoy it while you can, asshole, I thought.

"Ladies and Gentlemen of the Global Alliance," Burner cawed in greeting. "Let's dispense with the small

160

talk and get right down to business. I have in my possession eleven of your friends and family and I know you'd like to get them back, safe and sound."

The image on the screen changed from Burner's face to a wide shot of what looked like bleachers. Eleven people sat on those bleachers, duct tape stretched across their mouths. I leaned forward and quickly scanned the group. Candy was in the second row, her eyes wide with warring emotions: sheer terror and unrepentant anger.

Something in my chest suddenly swelled and went tight. I could feel the blood pumping in my arms. I had to bite my tongue to keep from crying out, from screaming in pure fury. Candy looked unhurt, but she was being held against her will and threatened with an ugly death. Somebody was going to pay dearly for that. More dearly than they ever imagined possible.

Burner's voice continued over the image of his hostages: "I am willing to sell the lives of all eleven of your esteemed loved ones for the one-time price of ten billion cashunits."

An audible cry went up among those in the war room. Burner didn't hear it ... or didn't care if he had.

"No negotiation, no haggling. Ten billion cashunits. If I don't have it in 24 hours, five of the people you see before you will enter the chamber here, one by one. That will leave us an even half dozen to sell later. At the same price, of course. No inventory reduction discounts." Burner smiled his friendly, boyish smile. I wanted to knock

161

every single tooth out of his mouth with a rusty bayonet.

The President stood up and addressed Burner's image. "Why?" He implored. "Why in God's name are you doing this?" His genuine bewilderment surprised and even touched me.

"Why?" Burner repeated, his eyes widening with obvious pleasure. "Why?" He snickered and shook his head, as though that was the stupidest questions he'd ever been asked. "Because I want the money, that's why." He touched a button on the console before him. "I'll be in touch with further instructions."

And the screen went blank again.

The room erupted in madness.

"Ten *billion* cashunits! There's no way ..."

"Twenty four hours isn't enough time ..."

"The man's insane!"

"There's got to be something we can do ..."

I let it all flow over me, like water over the proverbial goose's back, and instead concentrated on the red hot fury building inside of me.

Finally, the President began pounding his gavel for attention again. It was all but ignored. The pounding intensified in force and in intervals until finally, section by section, the enormous room quieted.

"Thank you for your attention," the President said irritably. He motioned toward General Dalton. "General?"

"I haven't heard from my tech people yet," Dalton answered. "But I don't think we had enough time, sir."

The President threw down his gavel in disgust. It clattered to the edge of the table, teetered there a moment, and then fell off onto the floor.

"So what do we do now?" someone in the mob cried out.

"We've got to pay the ransom!" somebody else said.

"We can't give in to a terrorist demand!" added yet someone else.

Sergeant Bruno tapped me on the shoulder. He pointed meaningfully to his forehead and said "Let's get the hell out of here."

We were almost to the door when Colin Hancock's voice rang out. "Mr. Fist!"

We kept walking.

"Mr. Fist!"

I glanced over at Bruno. We stopped and slowly turned back to face Hancock. The entire room was silent again and there was a sense of danger in the air.

"Where do you think you're going?" Hancock asked me.

"I'm going home," I told him.

"You'll stay here," Hancock said matter-of-factly. "You might be needed."

"I'm going home," I repeated. "My wife has been kidnapped by a goddamn terrorist and I don't have the stomach to sit around and watch you morons sign her death warrant."

Hancock's head jerked back as though he had been

slapped. "How dare you ..." he started. A faint rumble of outrage buzzed around the situation room. It simmered a moment, and then began to grow in volume. Before it became overwhelming once again, however, I heard the President mumble something unintelligible. After a moment, he repeated it, somewhat louder, and I could finally hear what he was saying.

"Let him go," the President said sadly, his shoulders sagging in defeat. Then, as the buzz of voices continued to rise, his voice grew louder still. "Let him go, I said. He's been through enough today."

I nodded at the President with gratitude, took one last look around the War Room, and then Bruno and I took our leave.

The elevator took us back up the 70 floors to street level and we stepped onto the marble walkway in the glaring afternoon sunlight. Bruno pointed out his 2159 Panzer DLX idling at the curb, its black surface shined to mirror perfection, its monster engine rumbling. I climbed in the back, Bruno took the driver's seat. I was near bursting with questions but held my tongue until we were safely under way. Within moments, we were airborne.

"So," I said to the person seated in the backseat beside me. "Did you find him?"

Iris Kessler of the Australian University of Higher Science gave me a quick, confident smile. Suddenly, that transparent dome and exposed brain of hers didn't seem so repulsive.

"I found him," she said. "I was right, Burner was using compressed TP waves to beam his transmissions into the White House."

"You can transmit audio and video signals using TP?" Bruno asked in wonder.

"And electricity, too," Kessler said. "I told you, Compressed TP is revolutionary."

"So that mega noggin of yours really works," I said. "Burner probably thought he had it made with Saunders out of the picture. No one knows compressed teleportation technology like Saunders did."

"But someone does now," Kessler said proudly. She clicked the side of her glass dome with a pen. "The extra memory and processing power my team installed helped me go through all his notes and research in about an hour and now I know as much about CTP as Saunders ever did."

"I can't thank you enough," I told her. "So, where is he?"

"He's closer than you think. Closer than any of us thought."

"Yeah? And where might that be?"

"According to my calculations," Iris Kessler said, "Burner's hiding on the far side of the moon."

CHAPTER TWENTY-ONE

I was beginning to feel like a galactic yo-yo, jumping back and forth from space to Earth and back to space again, but this time I didn't give a damn. We were on our way to the moon where, according to Iris Kessler, we would find Burner. And, if we found Burner, I was convinced I would also find Candy and the other Washington hostages.

I just hoped we found them in time.

Bruno's Panzer was a classic, but it didn't have the flexdrive speed of the Charger (may it rest in peace). Still, it was fast enough and we were well on our way.

"How close can you pinpoint his location?" I asked Kessler. She had insisted on coming along to the moon with us even though we made it clear how much danger she'd be in. There was no time to argue and I could only hope she'd be safe. So far, she'd proven to be one tough bird. A tough bird with an aquarium for a head, that is.

"Well, I can't tell you exactly," Kessler replied. "The far side is a mess. Since it's always facing away from the Earth, major corporations used it as a dumping site for centuries before the Alliance banned it. Practically the entire hemisphere is landfill. The few habitable areas there are like slums, where the low-paid workers live. But I can

166

get you within three or four miles, I think, based on the figures I ran when we did the trace."

I smiled at her appreciatively. "You did good," I said. She returned a smile of her own.

"You got a plan of action when we get where we're going?" Bruno asked from the front.

"Yeah," I told him. "Get Candy. Flapjack anyone that gets in my way."

"Flapjacking's too good for Burner," Bruno grumbled.

"You're right. But that's not up to me. He owes that debt to everyone." I swallowed. "Unless something happens to Candy. Then all bets are off."

"Ain't that the damn truth," Bruno agreed.

♣

A short time later, the luminescent expanse of the moon's surface filled the Panzer's windshield. As it continued to grow, I could see the first signs of mankind there - buoys advertising "Casino!" and "Eat!" floated past us; tour buses and other vehicles zipped to and fro; the geometric pixels of developed land began to form on the surface. Environmental domes began popping up like inverted dimples on a golf ball. Sometimes, we could even see people inside, going about their daily business.

But this was the near side of the moon and that wasn't our destination. Here, there were luxury casinos, 24-hour eateries and family attractions like roller coasters and

167

concert halls. Where we were going was the far side: a seemingly endless ocean of corporate garbage, shattered vehicles and nuclear waste. We were going to the side where bitter workers picked through the leftovers of the rich and cursed them at the same time they wished they could trade places with them.

Suddenly, as though a giant light switch had been thrown, we were past the corpulent vacation resorts and soaring, gaudy billboards and moving through hastily built shelters and rundown oxygen manufacturing plants. The environmental domes here were dirty and dingy and many were in sad states of repair. Although I'd heard that the far side of the moon actually gets more light than its opposite, our timing must have been off because the far side was now the dark side as well. Not only did the comfort of the light of day vanish but the temperature inside the Panzer seemed to drop by ten degrees. It was cold, grim and depressing.

"I haven't been here in twenty years," Kessler said, shivering a little. "I did a thesis on the destruction of the ecosystem here during my senior year in college and I took myself on a little field trip. I can't believe it hasn't changed in all these years."

"Destruction of the ecosystem?" Bruno asked. "It's the moon! What was there to destroy?"

"Oh, you'd be surprised, Mr. Bruno," said Kessler. "It may not have been an Amazonian rain forest here but there were things that we could have learned from. The

Corporations wiped them out before anyone had a chance to study them."

"Like what?" Bruno was not convinced.

"Like the Lunar Sand Devil," Kessler continued.

"The *what?*" I asked. Kessler laughed.

"The Lunar Sand Devil," she repeated. "It was a small, crustacean-like beetle that lived deep in the lunar soil. It had eye ridges that rose up over its eyes like horns, hence its name."

"And what was so special about this ... beetle?" Bruno asked.

"Have you ever seen a leech?" Kessler said.

"Of course."

"And you know what a leech does?"

"They drink blood."

"Actually, only some of them do, but you're right. They attach to their victim and remain attached, drawing blood, until they become full, then they drop off."

"Okay ..."

"Well, the Lunar Sand Devil did sort of the same thing," Kessler said, "Except that instead of drawing blood through its sucker, it drew disease."

"Disease?"

"Yes. It drew bacteria, viruses, infections ... I've even heard that it would draw cancer cells. Drew them into its body and, once it was full, it would simply drop off again."

"And what about the host?"

"They would become disease-free. The sand devil

absorbed and nourished itself on disease."

"I've never heard of anything like that," Bruno said.

"Neither have I," I added.

"Well, gentlemen, I've *seen* one," Kessler said. "And I can tell you they were real."

"Were?"

"Were. When the corporations started dumping their garbage here, the Sand Devils began dying off in hordes. By the time scientists realized their value it was too late to stop the extinction." Kessler paused a moment, sadly. "The last Sand Devil died in a laboratory on Earth three years ago."

"All in the name of the almighty cashunits," Bruno said.

As we all contemplated what could have been, a phrase in red light sprayed across the Panzer's windshield. "Nearing destination." I sat up in my seat.

"Okay, Iris," I said. "Help us find this bastard."

CHAPTER TWENTY-TWO

Using the coordinates she had triangulated on Earth and matching them to landmarks on the surface below us, Iris Kessler guided Bruno to a particularly grimy dome and said: "This is about the best I can do, gentlemen."

We pushed through the decrepit environmental dome entrance, entered the vehicular airlock and found ourselves in an industrial area, flush with warehouses, workshops and, of course, the neighborhood bar.

"Where shall we park?"

"Somewhere up high," Bruno said. "We need a good vantage point."

"How about there?" I pointed to the vacant roof of a three story building nearby.

"That should work," Bruno said and headed that way.

As Bruno eased the Panzer into its unauthorized parking space, I turned my attention to Kessler. "Listen," I said, "You've done more than enough just getting us here. I don't want you to take any unnecessary risks. The best thing for you to do is stay here in the car until we get back." She began to protest, but I pushed forward. "We'll lock it down in Armor mode and no one will be able to get in or at you. Plus, it's set to auto-return so, if something happens to us, you'll be taken back to Earth automatically in about five hours."

"But there must be something I can do to help," Kessler said.

"If there is, we'll be sure to ask," I told her. "But right now, we'll feel better if we know you're here, safe."

She pursed her lips and nodded in understanding. I could tell she would have gone along with us if we'd asked her, but I could also sense that she was relieved to stay behind where it was safe.

We left Kessler locked up in the limo and walked across the rooftop to the ledge overlooking the street. Our vantage point couldn't have been better. We could see the area surrounding us like a picture perfect panorama.

"Where do you think we should start?" I asked Bruno.

"Gotta be somebody here in charge," I said.

"You mean like in charge of the criminal element."

"Yeah. A gang leader or drug lord or something. Burner would have to recruit some temporary help in order to kidnap those people. If he's been here, the local crime scene would know it."

"So we start there," Bruno said, pointing to a broken, but still flashing, neon-light sign that read: "Lunartics Bar & Grill."

I nodded. "After you." We double checked to make sure Kessler was safely sealed away and then headed to the bar.

CHAPTER TWENTY-THREE

We started at Lunartics, of course, because bad guys always seem to hang out at bars and because I wanted a beer and a shot of tequila.

Lunartics was one of those cheesy, spacy dives that featured molded furniture, glasses shaped like beakers and lots of transparent plastic columns that were filled with liquid that constantly streamed with lines of air bubbles. The lighting was dim to hide the years of human grease that had rubbed off onto the furniture and a huge Stone Brewing Company sign advertised their latest creation: Empyrean Bastard Ale. The sign featured a leering, holographic demon who stared out over the patrons from behind the bar in a 3-D attempt to scare them into drinking the right beer.

The bartender was a compact man with a little hair on his head and a lot of hair on his lip. His brushy mustache seemed to reach out as though constantly trying to tickle something. He wore a pair of plain jeans and a black Amber Chapel t-shirt with no sleeves. The cigarette dangling out of his mouth threatened to fall out at any moment, its angry red tip glowing with single-minded malevolence.

"What can I getcha?" he mouthed around the smoke. His mustache danced dangerously near the fiery tip.

"Empyrean Bastard and a shot of Reyes Cartel tequila," I told him. "Anejo."

"Whiskey," Bruno said. "Maker's 226, if you got it."

"We got it."

As the bartender went about getting our beverages, I took a moment to survey the surroundings. Bruno did not. I knew he had already memorized the room, its exits and its occupants and sized them up for danger potential. I also knew by the level of his brow that nothing here concerned him.

Our drinks arrived and I took a big pull on my beer. It went down like roasted heaven, full and firm with a bold texture that actually had flavor rather than the watery crap they called beer these days. Bruno threw back his Maker's 226, swished it around in his mouth and pointed to the empty glass, telling the bartender, "Another."

I took a second gulp of beer and a sip of tequila and turned my back to the bar. The place was almost empty, as I'd expect it to be on a Wednesday night, but there were a few clumps of men sitting near the pool tables, staring glumly at the holographic balls and the "Out of Order" sign sitting near them. There were also two women in neon bright mini-skirts at a tall table, their skirts almost high enough for me to tell whether or not they were natural blonds and their ample chests all but spilling out from their low-cut tops. Occasionally, the depressed, bored men would glance sadly from the broken pool table to the brightly colored women and would either sigh in defeat or silently pray that one of the women would give them a wink and invite them to come over and introduce themselves.

They probably would have had better luck playing a game of pool on the broken table.

And then there was the table in the far corner, with two massive thugs sitting to the left and right of a tiny man with the face of an amphibian, whose beady black eyes stared out of his head like olives and whose chin had long since vanished into a cascading flow of alternate chins that spilled from his jaw like a fleshy waterfall.

The thugs were watching Bruno and me as well, us being the newest patrons of the bar, not to mention probably the only non-regulars here that evening.

I caught Bruno's eye. "Ya think?" I asked.

"Oh, yeah," he answered. "We've found the man in charge."

"Mob?"

"Maybe," Bruno said. "Maybe just a small-time crime lord."

"Think he knows anything about Burner?"

"One way to find out."

"Shall we?"

"Let's finish our drinks first," Bruno said, taking a sip of his third whiskey. "Then we can go say hi."

We downed our drinks, paid the man with the fluttering mustache, and stood up.

"Now, remember," I whispered to Bruno as we made

our way across the bar, "We need to get this information without too much of a fuss. We need to stay on the down low."

"Right."

We approached the crime lord's table and the two thugs bristled, their chests expanding to what looked like painful expanses. I raised my palm in a sign of peace. "We don't want any trouble," I said. "We're here to talk business."

One of the thugs turned to the crime lord to get his approval. The other never took his eyes off of us. With an almost imperceptible nod, the crime lord granted us access and the thugs' chests deflated slightly.

"Have a seat, gents," the crime lord said, using his eyebrows to indicate the two empty chairs opposite him. His voice fit his face. I was reminded of the legendary heavy metal singer Udo Dirkschneider, whose croaking vocal style was stunningly coarse and unique and, most importantly, effective. I was always surprised that, because of his intensity, Udo didn't die of a heart attack on stage during a live performance.

We took our seats and the crime lord looked us over for a few seconds. Finally, he said, "The name's Blatella. Carmine Blatella."

"My name is H.B. Fist," I said. "And this is my good friend, Sgt. Bruno."

Blatella made a disinterested shrugging motion. "So, what is it I can do for you gentlemen?"

"You can tell us where the fuck Burner is," Bruno said acidly. "You frog-faced piece of moon dirt."

With reflexes surprising considering their bulk, the two thugs simultaneously produced blazers from their shiny suits and had them pointed at Bruno and me. In the next second, however, they found themselves shockingly disarmed with Bruno pointing their own weapons back at them. I could tell from the pained look on their faces that their fingers were stinging from the unseen blow.

"Way to keep on the down low," I hissed at Bruno. He only grunted a response.

"What my friend meant to say ..." I said to Blatella. "... is would you gentlemen happen to know the whereabouts of the terrorist known as Burner?"

Blatella stared back at me, still wide-eyed with surprise at the way things were going down. "Who the hell are you guys?"

"We're recruiting new members for our barbershop quartet," Bruno spat. "Now answer the goddamn question."

"We're M.O.A.," I told Blatella, giving Bruno a hard glare. "We're working on the ZSW Memorial attack."

Blatella stared at us for what seemed a full minute, saying nothing. Finally, he shrugged. "Yeah, I know who you're talking about," he said. "He was here about three weeks ago. I rented him a shack up in the moonies."

"Moonies?" Bruno asked.

"Boonies," I told him. "On the moon."

Bruno gave a disgusted look.

"Is he there now?"

"No. I told you, he was there three weeks ago. It's just a storage unit."

"Storage unit? What kind of storage unit?"

Blatella crinkled his eyes. "A storage unit. You know, the kind where you store stuff."

"The kind of storage unit where someone could store illegal substances or machinery? Should they be so inclined."

"Yeah," Blatella said. "Should they be so inclined."

"How do we get to this unit?"

"I'll draw you a map. Take you right to it."

I looked at him suspiciously. "Why are you being so cooperative?"

"Look, when I rented the place to that guy, I had no idea who he was. Then, I see the news and I realize what this piece of shit had done. I don't go for that terrorist bullshit. I'm a man of business."

"Form of terror all its own," Bruno mumbled. Blatella ignored him.

"I may play a little rough with some of my clients, but I don't kill them, and I sure as hell don't kill innocent women and children. So, fuck him. You asked me where he was, I'll tell you."

"So why didn't you call this in earlier?"

"Plausible deniability. That kind of guy, finds out you dropped a dime on him, he'll kill you and your family ... and he'll do it slow and painful. But, when the M.O.A. shows up and beats it out of you ..."

He paused a moment to be sure we had digested what he meant. I nodded for him to go on.

"...well, even that kind of guy understands. He may not like it, but he understands."

Bruno nodded. "Now, how about that map?"

"Yeah, you got it." Blatella pulled a napkin over to him, slid a pen out of his pocket, and started drawing a series of intersecting lines and indicative arrows. After a few moments, he pushed it back across the table.

"It won't take you long to get there. We're here ..." he pointed at a spot on the map. "...and the unit is there." He tapped on another. "Two minutes by car, maybe thirty on foot."

"If this is a ruse ..." Bruno started.

"I don't think it is," I said, watching Blatella. "I appreciate you doing the right thing here."

"Got nothing to do with right and wrong," Blatella said. "I just want that guy to go down."

Bruno and I stood and thanked Blatella again. Bruno returned the thugs' weapons with a glance that told them to put them away and keep them out of sight. We were walking away from the table toward the exit when Blatella called out to us one last time. "Hey, if he ain't there, maybe that crazy broad he's with will be."

We stopped. "Crazy broad?" I asked.

"Yeah, a real wild one," Blatella continued. "Got like a

179

fishbowl for a head or somethin'. Some kind of doctor or scientist or somethin'. Nice lookin' broad if it weren't for the globe."

Bruno and I exchanged slow, stunned glances.

"Remember her name?" I asked him, as if there could be any doubt.

"Whistler, I think," Blatella said. "No, it's, uh, Kistler? Nah, that ain't right. Somethin' like that, though."

"Kessler," I said flatly.

"Yeah, Kessler!" Blatella snapped his fingers and pointed at me. "That's it!"

Bruno and I went back to the bar and ordered another drink. That quickly, all of our plans had changed.

CHAPTER TWENTY-FOUR

Bruno and I came out of Lunartics and stopped in front of the flashing sign. It bathed us in red light, then white, red light, then white. I gave a brief wave in the direction of the Panzer, pulled out my handcom and called Kessler.

"Iris, we're off to follow a lead. If we're not back in an hour, get the hell out of here."

"Be careful, Mr. Fist."

"We will. You do the same." I closed the handcom and gave her another little wave. Then, Bruno and I walked away.

Twenty five minutes later, Kessler sat in the Panzer, anxiously staring out at the grey horizon. Suddenly, she stiffened with shock as a great ball of flame blossomed in the distance. Her shoulders sagged with what seemed to be relief. The booby trap had been tripped. The bomb had exploded.

H.B. Fist and Sgt. Bruno were dead.

She touched the side of her head where her temcom was implanted and spoke quickly and quietly to someone on the other end. She disconnected the call, slid into the driver's seat and powered up the Panzer.

Well, she *tried* to power up the Panzer. But the Panzer wouldn't start because the flex drive stem was in my hand

and not in the flex drive unit like it should have been.

I stepped over to the window and rapped gently on the glass.

Kessler jumped, turned and stared at me in wide-eyed wonder that quickly faded to a quiet kind of horror.

"Iris," I said. "We need to talk."

I cuffed her and marched her over to a nearby warehouse on loan to us from Carmine Blattela. It was a rusting steelcore building that had been slapped together with staples and glue and looked like it would blow over at the slightest breeze.

Bruno had returned from his field trip to set off the booby trap and was now sitting about six feet away from the handcuffed Kessler, trying to kill her with his most penetrating glare. To her credit, she didn't seem too frightened.

"Mr. Bruno ..." she started.

"That's *Sergeant* to you."

"Sergeant Bruno. If you're attempting to frighten me, I'm afraid you're wasting your time. I had full awareness of what I was doing and the consequences thereof. And I am willing to accept them."

"Had my way, you'd hang."

"But you *don't* have your way, do you?"

"Don't be too sure."

"You know, Iris," I said. "There's actually a bit of truth to that. See, normally, my friend Bruno and I, we have the laws of the Global Alliance behind us. And, generally, we follow them to the letter. Violence comes to us in our duties, make no mistake about it, but we've never killed an eleven year old girl because we wanted some extra spending money or because we disagreed with her religious or political views."

"Or because she happened to be in our way," Bruno added.

"Your boyfriend, Burner, on the other hand..."

"He is *not* my boyfriend," Kessler corrected firmly.

"Whatever he was to you, Iris, we don't give a shit about him, his beliefs or his life. He's killed and terrorized too many people and, personally, I can't wait to flapjack his ass and get him filed away on Shatner's planet. If I have to put him in the ground instead, well, this is one of those times I won't mind doing that, either."

"Amen, brother," Bruno chanted.

Kessler stared at me disinterestedly.

I wanted to smash her glass-topped head in.

Launching myself out of the chair, I grabbed Kessler's shoulders and pressed my nose flush against hers. I wasn't playacting any more. The rage was surging out of me like a tangible energy.

"Your friend, your spiritual advisor, or whatever the fuck he is to you ... well, he took my wife this time, Iris. Kidnapped her. And threatened to kill her. And right now, Iris, right now, I don't give a rat's ass about the Alliance's code of ethics. All I care about is getting my wife back and I'll do whatever it takes to get her."

183

I forced myself away and sat back, staring hard into Kessler's eyes. She was still trying to stay tough, but I could see the first cracks of her breaking down.

"You don't frighten me," she said weakly.

"Good. Then we understand one another. I'll ask you once, Iris, to please remove your temcom and place it in the palm of my hand."

"I can't do that," Kessler whispered.

"As you wish," I told her. Then I stood up, drew back my hand and slapped her across the face. Hard. Her brain spattered against its glass dome, pressing flat for a moment before falling back into place. My palm stung where it had connected with her face, the tips of my fingers vibrated where they'd met the edges of her globe and the crimson image of my palm glowed across her cheek.

Kessler stared at me for a split second, shocked, horrified and reeling with pain.

And then she began to cry.

Not the gentle tears of a jilted lover but the kind of gut-wrenching sobbing that came from down deep, from somewhere that hadn't been accessed for many, many years. Tears and snot flowed down her face and her breath came in great painful hitches.

"You son of a bitch!" she screamed at me in unbridled fury, spots of blood spraying from her lips. But then, almost instantly, the fury seemed to seep out of her and she said again, more quietly: "You son of a bitch. I can't tell you. I can't! He'll kill her."

She took another deep, hitching breath, shook her head gently, and the sobbing continued in earnest.

I stared down at her for a moment as a sickening realization dawned on me. "Who?" I asked her. "He'll kill who?"

"Deidra," Kessler said. She took yet another deep breath and let it out in painful sobs. "My wife. Burner kidnapped my wife, too. He said if I didn't do what he asked, he'd kill her."

I fell back into the chair behind me. It felt like I'd just been punched hard in the gut. "I'm sorry," I said. "I didn't know."

It was less than a whisper: "You son of a bitch."

"Iris, listen to me," I said, sitting forward. "I am sorry. I had no idea you were going through the exact same thing I am and I apologize for putting you through all this. But I need your help here, Deidre needs your help here. Trust me, I know this man and he will kill both of our wives if we don't stop him first."

With the word "kill," Kessler began sobbing anew.

"If you give me your temcom, I can trace Burner's call back to his location."

"Those types of calls aren't traceable," Kessler mumbled.

"Not by the general public, no," I said. "But I'm M.O.A. I have the means to trace them."

For the first time, Kessler looked up hopefully. "Can you save her?"

"I think I can."

"Can you promise me that?"

I shook my head. "No. But I can promise you I will do my best. And I can promise you that Burner has no intention of ever releasing her himself."

"You have to promise me," Kessler said. "You have to promise me you'll save Deidre first."

"I can't..."

"You have to!" Kessler's voice raised dangerously. "You have to promise me you'll save her first!" She stared at me with a teary-eyed intensity that told me there was no negotiating this point.

I glanced at the clock on the wall. I was running out of time. Fast.

"All right," I told her reluctantly, "I promise I'll save Deidre first." Bruno looked at me questioningly. I gave him a small, what-was-I-supposed-to-do shrug.

Kessler's shoulders and face relaxed as relief flooded over her. I felt a little pang of guilt at my half-meant promise.

And, of course, the bright red images of my fingers across her face.

"I can't give you my temcom," Kessler told me. "It's hard-wired. Because of this." She rapped her knuckles against her glass forehead, a little too hard, angrily. The contents sloshed and jiggled.

"Well," I said. "I can still take it. But it will be painful."

"I don't care," Kessler told me. "I just want my Deidre

back."

I reached back with an open palm and Bruno slapped a tool into it. A flathead screwdriver, its edge sharpened to a near razor point. "I'm gonna have to cut it out, Iris. And it's going to hurt. A lot. The only anesthesia we have is this bottle of tequila ..." I pressed a bottle of Reyes Cartel into her hand. "... but it's not going to mask the pain much. I wish we had more time to do this properly, but ..."

"Just cut the fucking thing out already," Kessler spat.

So I did.

CHAPTER TWENTY-FIVE

Temcoms are buried just beneath the skin so that they're very easy to remove in the event they need to be replaced or repaired. They're supposed to be removed only by technicians who know what they're doing, however, or there can be irreparable damage not only to the device but to the person who's wearing it.

And, in this case, the removal would be further complicated by hardwiring instead of wireless technology.

But again, we were running out of time, and both Kessler and I knew it.

It took me about 60 seconds to pry Kessler's temcom out of her head, all the while with her screaming loudly in horrendous pain and cursing the existence of me, my parents and the act they had committed in order to create me. Soon enough, I had the device in my hands and Kessler was finally silent, thanks to the warm, blessed blanket of unconsciousness.

"Patch her up, would ya?" I asked Bruno.

"Roger," he said.

I left Bruno to bandage the hole I'd dug in the side of Kessler's head while I went into the next room where Carmine and his bulging thugs waited. They looked at me with a newfound respect that I did not relish.

"Companel?"

"Next room," Carmine said. "On the wall."

I found the companel, signed in and located the port. I plugged the temcom into the port and a waterfall of Kessler's life appeared before me. Family photos, video from happier times, hundreds of cascading numbers and names.

Many images of a black-haired woman I assumed was Deidre, her wife.

I dug through the collage of pixeled light images and made my way directly to the last call the temcom had made. As I suspected, Burner has insisted Kessler call him after the bomb in the shed had gone off, to let him know the deed was done.

Unfortunately for Burner, reports of our deaths were greatly exaggerated.

I found the last call and pulled up the telecom I.D. file. A fresh-faced man in a business suit stared back at me. I knew it wasn't Burner but was probably the photo that came with his wallet when he bought it. I slid the photo aside and found a number hidden beneath.

This was the serial number of the telecom that Burner had used when he last spoke to Kessler. I was getting close.

I grabbed the number and slid it into a reader. The words "No Record Found" blinked back at me. I wasn't surprised. Burner wasn't stupid. He probably had several layers of protection between the serial number of his telecom and the information I needed to find out where he was.

But he didn't have what I had. I tapped the serial

number with my fingertips and it glowed, highlighted there, floating in the air. I opened a window across the center of it and then entered one of Boris's secret info codes. This time, an address shot out.

1600 Pennsylvania Avenue Northwest. Washington, D.C.

The White House.

Nice try, I thought. Burner's sense of humor at work.

I snatched the address out of the air, inserted it yet again into the reader, entered another of Boris's magic codes, and waited. The code I entered was another cipher that would break down the fake address and display the real one.

But the same address came back again.

1600 Pennsylvania Avenue Northwest. Washington, D.C.

I opened up a map of the world and entered Burner's telecom I.D. into the reader. Another one of Boris's codes followed, this one which would show me exactly where Burner's telecom was at this very moment. If he was on Earth, this would find him. He could build layer upon layer of protection and feed us fake addresses all day long, but there was no security anywhere that Boris's codes couldn't get through. I stared at the map of the world and waited for the telltale pinpoint to light up, indicating the very spot where I could find Burner, or at the very least his telecom.

The pinpoint came up quickly and I expanded it for easy viewing on the map.

1600 Pennsylvania Avenue Northwest. Washington, D.C.

This was no fake address. Burner was actually somewhere at the White House. Talk about hiding in plain sight.

Suddenly, my own handcom buzzed. I snatched it out of my pocket. "Fist," I said.

"H.B., it's Boris," my old friend said in a shockingly flat tone. "I've got some bad news."

CHAPTER TWENTY-SIX

In the past, when a loved one was in peril, I have always felt anger. Anger that led me to take action. Anger that gave me the strength to go above and beyond the call of duty, to do what I need to do to take the problem head on and to make things right, whatever the cost.

But, now, as I stared at the image on the screen that Boris had just sent me, I felt a cold emptiness drop over me. An emptiness that was alive with deadly energy. A feeling as though someone had just disemboweled me with a knife of solid, polar ice.

Because on the screen was a video shot of Candy, dressed in one of those ordinary jump suits, standing in the very same retort chamber that Colin Marlow had died in. Her hands were tied behind her back and her eyes stared straight forward with chilly, venomous defiance.

A timer in the lower right corner of the screen continued to tick down. It was now at 56 minutes and dropping.

"We received this about five minutes ago," Boris informed me. "With another demand for ten billion cashunits. H.B. ... I'm sorry."

"Tell me that when I see you," I told him. "I'm coming home."

"There's nothing you can do here," Boris said. "We still don't have any fix on his location. And you know we can't negotiate...."

"No," I said simply. "No negotiating."

"H.B., by the time you get here ... well, it may not matter anymore."

"I've got information that says otherwise, Boris. Just keep this between you and me for the moment. I'll be there shortly."

Boris gave a deep sigh and looked back at me soberly. "I'll do whatever you need me to do, H.B.," he said. "Just name it."

We logged off.

"If anything happens to her, I will kill that cocksucker personally," Bruno said behind me. I hadn't even realized he had come in. "And then I'll have him cloned so I can kill him again and again. And I will make his last moments of each of his lives an unimaginable hell."

"Nothing's going to happen to her," I said. "We've got to get back to Earth, like now. How's Iris?"

"Drugged. She'll be out for a few hours at least."

"Load her up. We might need her."

"Is Burner really at the White House?"

"It appears that way."

"Probably in the tunnels underneath," Bruno said soberly. "H.B., there's hundreds of miles of them."

"Yeah, but how many of those retort chambers are there?"

"Probably not too many," Bruno said.

"And why are they there in the first place?"

"You don't want to know."

"No. Probably not," I admitted.

"We don't have time to search them all," Bruno said plainly.

"Maybe we won't have to.

"You know something I don't?"

"Maybe."

"Maybe? *Maybe*? What's with all these maybes?"

"It's all we've got, old friend."

"So where are we off to?"

"We're going back to school."

CHAPTER TWENTY-SEVEN

We packed the unconscious Kessler – with the half-assed bandage Bruno had made wrapped around her glass dome – into the Panzer and Bruno pushed the classic car to its limits. We were back to Earth in less than twenty minutes and made up some more time by skipping the daycab trip and taking the Panzer directly to Iris Kessler's office.

Kessler's assistant, the cool but attractive Sandra Jimenez, looked up at us with widened eyes, startled to see our reappearance there. She did a double-take as she looked at her bloodied boss hanging over Bruno's shoulder.

"What have you done to her!" Sandra cried, standing and pressing her palms to her face in horror.

"Don't worry about her," I told her. "We need to get into Saunders' lab now."

"You've been all through his office ..."

"Not his office. His *lab*. Where he did all his work. There was no time to search it last time we were here. We had a bit of an emergency, as you might remember."

"I'm not sure ..." She eyed Kessler's limp form.

"Now is not the time, sister," I snapped. "Unless you want to end up like your boss here, you'll take us to that lab right this second." I conveniently left out the part that her boss had come to this condition on her own accord.

"No," Sandra said. "Something's not right. I'm calling the police.'

I pulled out the flapjacker and pressed it against the side of her head. "I *encourage* you to call the police," I told her. "Right after you take us to Saunder's lab."

Staring from the flat empty eye of the flapjacker to the bloody bandage wrapped around her boss's head, Sandra finally acquiesced. As she put down the phone, Bruno laid the still unconscious Iris Kessler on a couch in the waiting room and we followed Sandra as she guided us down a few corridors, through a few hallways and down a few staircases. Eventually, we came to a door marked:

Dr. Donald Saunders

LAB

"I don't have a key," Sandra said upon our arrival.

"That's all right," I told her, "We won't be needing one. Now, go run and call the police if that'll make you feel better."

She didn't need to be asked twice. I glanced at my watch. Fifteen minutes were all that Candy had remaining.

"Are you sure about this?" Bruno asked.

"As sure as I am about anything," I told him. "Burner had to have a CTP portal here somewhere in order to beam himself from place to place."

"Why here?"

"Where else? He had the tools, the cover, the power and the people. Right here. Where else could he have done it?"

"That's a good point."

"And, if he used compressed TP to swap himself out with the android on Kronos and to get past the ZSW Memorial security, he probably also used it ..."

"...to get past White House security!"

"Which means, of course, if we're lucky..." I grinned a malignant grin. "...the teleporter is still set to those coordinates."

"...and we can beam ourselves over and take the fucker out."

"That's what I'm thinking."

Of course the lab door was locked but there hasn't been a door made that Sgt. Bruno couldn't open in thirty seconds or less. In half that time, the lock clicked and the door swung open. Bruno's sterling reputation as a lock pick remained untarnished.

"What are we looking for?" Bruno said, peering into the lab.

"Hell if I know."

"We should have asked Kessler," Bruno said.

"Take too long to wake her up and get her up to speed," I said. "And she might not know anything anyway. Look for something big, like a booth or a chair or something like that."

We spread out. The lab was vast and sloppy. Equipment was littered throughout like a child's toys scattered throughout his room.

I glanced at my timepiece again. Ten minutes.

"We're running out of time!" I said. I had to.

No response from Bruno. Then: "Hey! What's this?"

I darted over to where Bruno was standing over what looked like a deep old-fashioned bathtub. It was a white porcelain canoe-like structure surrounded with a perimeter of electrodes. A series of nozzles pointed down into the glistening bowl. I ran my fingers over a big red pushbutton attached to the side, its glowing red LED readout displaying a string of numbers that meant nothing to me, and a quartet of dials set into an onboard console.

"What do you think?" Bruno asked.

"I would guess that this is the Engage button, and that the readout is the coordinates of the destination." I stared at the dials for a moment and then snapped my fingers. "And I'll bet that's a timer."

"A timer?"

"Sure. Burner can't have these devices spread out all over the planet. The timer is set so that, after a pre-determined amount of time, he'll be automatically returned here."

Bruno nodded. "Makes sense."

I glanced at my watch. Six minutes.

What choice did I have? I climbed in.

"You can't go in alone," Bruno said. "He's going to have help. You know he had to recruit a small army in order to kidnap all those people."

"I know."

"So how do you expect to take them all down before

he does Candy?"

"I don't know."

"There's bound to be a dozen people between you and him," Bruno said. "They'll cut you down before you even get halfway there."

A little light flashed on in my brain.

"Did you bring that tin of yours?" I asked.

"What tin?" Bruno asked. Then his shoulders sagged. "You mean the Stathe?"

"Yeah. The Stathe."

"Yeah, I got it," Bruno said, reaching into his pocket. "You sure you want to do this?"

"No. I'm not." I took the tin from his hand, pried open the lid, and scooped two fingers down deep into the bowl. A chunk the size of a tablespoon came out. I brushed it across my upper gums and teeth, then repeated the action with another tablespoon on my lower teeth. Instantly, my jaw began to tingle. The tingling ran from my jaw to my feet and back again. An electric charge shot through my entire body.

"Jesus," Bruno said. "That shit's gonna kill you."

"Not me," I said, lowering myself into the bathtub. "But somebody's gonna die." My mouth felt like I had just eaten a bowl of jalapenos, and my clothes suddenly felt tighter, as though my arms and legs were swelling. I pointed at the big red button. "Push it."

"H.B., you can't go in alone," Bruno said angrily.

"Push the fucking button," I told him. "The worst it

199

can do is kill me. And, if Candy dies, that won't matter anyway." My arms were twitching now, the muscles rippling with a new, electric power. The room around me seemed to focus into sharper details. Colors were brighter. Lines were cleaner. I felt bigger, stronger, faster, meaner.

I felt invincible.

Bruno still hesitated. I looked at him imploringly. "Please, Bruno, push the goddamn button."

"Aw, shit," Bruno said.

And he pushed the goddamn button.

CHAPTER TWENTY-EIGHT

It was only a matter of seconds but, to me, it felt like days. The tingling sensation of the Stathe merged with the prickly sensation of teleportation and I felt as though I was *vibrating* through space and time. At one second, I was H.B. Fist, man of action, mercenary for the Global Alliance, deep in the bowels of the Australian University for High Science. And the next I was a raging killing machine, nearly ten thousand miles away.

I opened my eyes to find myself in what seemed to be a basement lit brilliantly with dozens of spotlights hanging from the low ceiling. Two men stood over me, their eyes wide-eyed in shock and surprise, their sidearms drawn but not quite ready. A pair of massive hands, which couldn't have been my hands because they were *huge* hands that rippled and bulged with cable-like muscles and pulsing veins, reached out and grabbed the men by the sides of their heads and crushed them together, their skulls exploding like eggs filled with rancid cranberry dressing.

And I realized they *were* my hands. The Stathe had worked its awful magic.

I was aware of voices, live and electronic, droning on in another part of the building as a third man stepped out from behind a door, the old school machine laser rifle in his hands spitting deadly bullets of light at me. But I was too quick for his aim and was beside him before he knew it, shoving him behind the door and using it to crush the life out of him. A crimson tsunami washed out from beneath the door and I moved on.

The next man came at me from behind, trying to lever his forearm around my throat to choke me into submission. He squealed in high-pitched terror as I ripped that arm from its socket and wielded it like a nightstick, beating the man to the ground with his own knuckles and bloody fingers.

I was getting closer to the droning voices. There was some hesitation to their words now. They hadn't stopped but they were continuing haltingly, as though the speaker was aware that something was wrong but could not comprehend what it could possibly be.

I continued to rage through room after room, pulling doors off of their hinges, overturning tables, bursting through walls as though they were paper. My body continued to vibrate as though powered by high voltage and I felt bigger, stronger, more deadly than I ever had before. I was aware of several cuts and bruises on my body and face but they weren't important. Only the mission was important and anyone or anything that got in my way was going to be completely and utterly destroyed. As if to prove that point, another terrorist suddenly broke cover and came right at me. I thrust out my fist in time with his forward motion and my knuckles crushed his jaw to powder as my arm slid up to the wrist into his throat. I opened my hand inside, grabbed what felt like pumpkin innards, and yanked. His body jerked once and then went limp forever.

They kept coming at me and I kept knocking them back. The patina of blood on my hands grew thick and syrupy. The floor was wet with black/red liquid. Strings of skin, muscle and sinew hung from between my fingers. Sharp pieces of other men's bone jutted from my knuckles and fists. My mouth tasted of blood and, horribly, I knew it wasn't my own.

A trail of bodies piled up behind me. And still I moved forward.

Finally, I burst into the room the voices had been coming from. It was like a television studio, with bright lights glaring down everywhere. The wall in front of me was a giant companel and I realized I had arrived in the middle of the latest Burner broadcast.

The *last* Burner broadcast.

On the panel in front of me was an image of the War Room, where the video faces of the President and the others stared at me with numbing shock and unbridled horror.

And standing in the room with his back to me, his orange hair actually a little mussed for once, was Burner. He spun away from the companel to face me and his jaw dropped in shock and his eyes widened in horror as he looked into my blood-splashed face and at my gore-painted hands.

And he defiantly held up a small remote control device

203

set with a single button.

"I don't know who the hell you are," he said. "But you're too late."

And he pushed the button. And then ran out of the room.

I started to go after him and then forced myself to stop, taking in my surroundings. My head buzzed and spun with the effects of the Stathe.

I looked to my left. There was a glass doored retort chamber there where ten hostages stood watching, their faces masks of wild terror.

I turned to my right. Another chamber was there, where Candy stood alone, her face a twisted combination of fear, cautious relief and unconditional concern.

A deep thrum ran through the floor as some huge machinery began to work and my skin bristled as the chambers on both sides of me began to glow with heat. I glanced at the ten people on the left, and then at Candy on the right. Instinctively, I headed toward the chamber with Candy...

...And then I looked over my shoulder to the chamber with the ten others. And I saw Deidre there in the front. Clutching her cheeks in terror, her face streaked with tears, sweat pouring off of her face and neck.

And I remembered my promise.

I turned to the left and I ran to the chamber and I slammed my fist down on the bright red killswitch. I waited a painful second while it turned from deadly red to safety green and I watched for an eternity as the walls faded from orange to yellow to their original cool blue. Then I leapt over to the chamber on the right and my heart stopped as I saw Candy on the floor, her hair splayed out in an amber wave, her jumpsuit soaked through with sweat, and the walls glowing a fiery red and I pounded the glowing killswitch, waited an even longer eternity until it turned green, and then nearly ripped the door off the chamber and dropped down by Candy's side.

Her eyes fluttered up at me as I turned her over, the blood of my victims dripping down onto her cheek, and she looked up at me and said, "H.B.? Is that really you?"

I kissed her forehead softly, leaving a bloody set of lip prints there, and I set her down gently and raced back the way I came. Back over the piles of torn and ripped bodies, back through the destruction I had wreaked thanks to a tin full of Statham 666, and finally I found myself in the room I had first arrived here in, the room with the TP machine, and I found Burner there in the tub, pounding the now useless button that I had smashed to bits upon my arrival, staring up at me with total, abject and utterly *satisfying* terror as my now mutated hands, swollen with power and hungry for death reached out and wrapped around his tiny, insignificant throat...

...And although I had never wanted anything more than to throttle the life out of him there and then, I knew that it wasn't my place to do it. My job was nearly done here and, through the haze of Stathe that had turned me into a monster, I reached back into the holster and pulled out the flapjacker. And I turned that terrorist motherfucker into celluloid.

The flat yellow beam hit him in the chest and enveloped him like a malignant fog. He screamed in pain, or tried to, as the beam went about its work of converting him from a three dimensional living being into a two dimensional wall hanging. After a moment, the final, sickeningly sticky wet pop burst the silence and Burner's flapjack cel lay before me on the floor. He was no longer a man. Now, he was only a life-sized photo of himself that could cause no more harm to anyone.

I snatched the cel off the floor rolled it into a tube, cramming it into my back pocket. Then, I turned and made my way back into the chamber room.

The video images of the people in the War Room stared wide-eyed back at me from the companel wall screen as I re-entered. They looked at me as though I were some fierce animal, unloosed at the zoo and wreaking havoc on the humans that were nearby.

And they weren't too far from the truth.

"Mr. Fist," the President said, his voice husky at the carnage he had witnessed. "What is the status ..."

I reached out and switched off the companel. The screen went black. The hostages gathered around me, naturally yearning to be near their savior. One of them pushed through the others and fell into my arms.

Candy.

My mind was hazy from the effects of the drug. I felt as though I were in someone else's body, staring out through someone else's eyes. I wanted nothing more than to pass out and to wake up later when this was all over. But I wasn't about to leave Candy's side.

Not again.

Not ever.

I gave my wife another kiss, leaving a second bloody rosebud on her cheek, and we waited for the cavalry to arrive.

CHAPTER TWENTY-NINE

An hour later, it was all over. The hostages were gathered up and taken elsewhere for clean-up and debriefing. I didn't want Candy to go but, of course, she insisted. Sgt. Bruno was en route back from Australia and I was in Boris's White House office, enjoying a big tumbler of Reyes Cartel over ice. Every once in a while, when I shifted, I could hear the crinkling of Burner's flapjacker cel in my back pocket. Although I doubted he felt any discomfort, it gave me no small satisfaction knowing that I had him pinned between the seat cushion and my ass.

I had taken a few moments to clean up myself. I was sore in places I never knew could be sore and my head was still spinning with the effects of the Stathe. I hurt now but I knew it was *really* going to hurt in the morning. The Reyes helped but only a little.

The door opened and Boris wheeled in, his enormous girth sagging dangerously on the support rods and dollies. In his hands were two of the biggest cigars I'd ever seen.

"I'd say you earned one of these," he said, handing me a stogie twice as big around as my finger.

"Whether I did or not, I'll take one," I told him. He stuck the cigar in my mouth and lit it while I puffed. The smoke was wondrous, deep, heavy and savory. I nodded my thanks to Boris who wheeled away to take his place behind his giant desk.

"The President is so pleased," Boris said. "He's going to award you yet another medal."

"Yippee. Did he say how pleased he was when I hung up on his ass downstairs?"

"No, he didn't like that," Boris admitted. "But what's he going to do? Stay angry at the man who took down Burner?"

"Don't care," I said.

"Anyways, I think he's a little scared of you. That was quite some show you put on for them."

"Every once in a while they need to see what war's really like," I said. "Make them think twice about getting into it."

Boris puffed out a gray cloud of smoke. "Where's the cel?" he asked.

"Back pocket." When I said "pocket," the puff of air made a spark fly from my cigar and float gently to the rug where it flared briefly and then quickly died out.

"May I see it?" Boris asked. I knew he meant "take it" but I reached for it anyway.

"So what's the plan here?"

"Plan?"

"Yeah. What are they doing with his cel?"

Bruno looked at me curiously. "Why, they're sending it to Shatner's Planet, of course, for storage."

"I'm not so sure I like that."

"What do you mean?"

"I mean, this fucker killed over three thousand people

this week. He tried to kill thousands more. And, he kidnapped my wife."

Boris's face grew grim. "Yes, I know."

"And that doesn't include all the others he's killed over the years, or anyone he's maimed or terrorized before today. How many more is that? Ten thousand? Twenty? The entire fucking universe?"

Boris nodded sadly. "I know," he said. "I know."

"And what if he escapes again?"

"He won't escape from Shatner's Planet."

"DemiGod did."

Boris nodded again. "Yes, that's true. But what's your point, H.B.?"

"My point is that I'd rather he was gone forever than filed in some metal box under B for Burner."

"Well, I don't disagree, but the law is the law. Flap-jacked criminals go to Shatner's Planet."

"Yeah, I know," I grumbled. "But I don't have to like it." I frowned. "Hey, my smoke burned out. Throw me that light, will ya?"

Boris tossed the lighter to me. I caught it, hit the jet, lit up the stogie and then kept the fire going as I held out the flapjacker cel and put the flame to the edge. I watched with macabre delight as the thing began to burn.

"H.B.! What are you doing?!" Boris cried.

"Oops," I said. "Guess I got too close."

"You can't do that!"

"I said 'oops.'" The cel burned bright with an orange-blue flame and then curled into a black ribbon. The room was filled with a sour, acrid stench that reminded me of barbequed chicken and burning plastic. Just as the flames reached my fingertips, I dropped the remains of the cel at my feet and stomped out the embers.

"Damn," I said. "What a shame."

Boris stared back at me with a look of horror, distaste and disbelief plastered onto his features.

As the smoking ruins of Burner crumbled into a smear of gray ash, I leaned down and blew it all away. I took another puff of the cigar Boris had given me and winked at him.

"Good smoke, no?"

CHAPTER THIRTY

I was at the front of the line as the shuttle carrying the debriefed hostages came to rest amidst a huge crowd of paparazzi. For once, the press wasn't interested in me. The President and his staff had decided that it was probably best to play down my part in stopping Burner, especially since their "Just Say No to Stathe" campaign had begun just two months before.

I counted six people before Candy appeared at the shuttle door. Her big hazel eyes searched for me, found me and seconds later she was in my arms, my face buried in her auburn hair.

"How was your interview?" I asked.

"Softball questions," Candy replied. "The debriefing was easy. But, God, it felt good to take a shower."

We were quiet a moment and then Candy said, "I knew you'd save the day."

"We got lucky."

Candy looked up at me seriously. "No. Luck had nothing to do with it."

I pulled her close again.

"I do have one question," Candy said with a tone of mock accusation.

"Yes?"

"When you came into the chamber room ... why'd you open the other chamber first?"

"Noticed that, did ya?"

"Kinda hard not to."

"Well ..." I said slowly. "I promised someone I would."

"You promised?"

"Yeah."

"Oh," Candy said simply. "And here I thought it was something noble, like, you know, there were more people in that room than my room and the needs of the many outweigh the needs of the few. Something like that."

"Nope," I said. "Just keeping a promise."

"Well, you can't break a promise."

"No, you can't," I agreed.

We stood there a moment, just enjoying being together. Finally, we pulled apart and started walking toward the Panzer. Bruno had loaned it to me for the day.

"Where's the Charger?" Candy asked, her cute little brow wrinkling in puzzlement.

"That's a long story," I said. "I'll tell you over dinner. With all this excitement, I feel like I haven't eaten in days."

"When's the last time you ate?" Candy asked.

"It's been days."

"H.B.!"

"How about pizza?" I asked her. "And beer?"

Candy made a face. "No beer for me. They have wine?"

"They do."

"Then pizza it is."

I looked up at the bluing Ventura sunset, its stakes of

sunlight reaching toward the heavens while its warm glow turned the Pacific Ocean into liquid gold.

We climbed into the Panzer. I started its mammoth engine.

"You're not going to have any pizza, are you?" I asked her.

Candy looked at me slyly. "I really only want a glass of wine."

"That's okay," I told her. "I really only want a beer."

"See?" Candy said. "Made for each other."

And we headed off into the night sky.

ABOUT THE AUTHOR

R. Scott Bolton lives in Ventura with his wife Shelley, his son Josh and his dogs, Leo and Zoey. He hosts internet radio shows for fun and you can listen to them by visiting his internet radio station at www.RoughEdgeFM.com.

Scott loves hearing from readers and welcomes e-mails at rsb@rscottbolton.com.